Return
of the
Wulfhedinn

BOOK TWO
OF THE WULFHEDINN SERIES

Return
of the
Wulfhedinn

CATHERINE SPADER

QUILLSTONE
PRESS

LITTLETON, CO

Return of the Wulfhedinn – Book Two of the Wulfhedinn Series
Published by Quillstone Press
Littleton, CO

Library of Congress Control Number: 2017948709

Spader, Catherine, Author
Return of the Wulfhedinn – Book Two of the Wulfhedinn Series
Catherine Spader

ISBN: 978-0-9971535-3-8
Cover design by Nick Zelinger at NZ Graphics

Fantasy / Historical

QUANTITY PURCHASES: Schools, companies, professional groups, clubs, and other organizations may qualify for special terms when ordering quantities of this title. For information, email info@ quillstonepress.com.

LITTLETON, CO

For Craig,

The bear who embraces the wolf in me
May we stay well fed with all that feeds us.

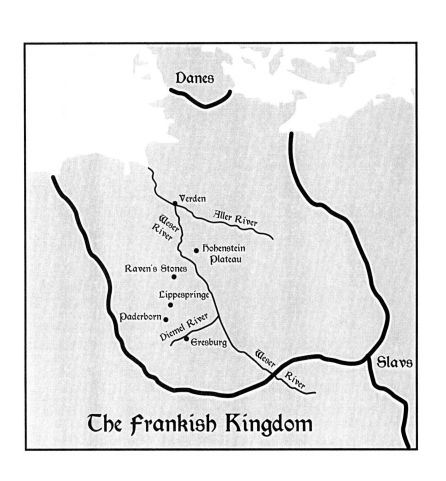

The Frankish Kingdom

A Hunt for Prey

Saxony, 782 AD

I ran as if I had four legs. I no longer wore the wolf skin on my back, but I ran like the beast, the demon, the Wulfhedinn.

The woodland air was fresh and crisp. It smelled of freedom.

The soft earth felt so different under my bare feet than the stone floor of the chamber where I had been caged. I sprinted until my legs cramped with fatigue, but I pushed through the pain. Branches whipped past my face, and thorns scratched my arms and legs. My chest heaved for more air. I was not as strong as I had been, but I had escaped the Saxon witch, the Walkyrie.

Galloping across the skies
On her black stallion
Soaring on the black wings of the Raven
The Eater of Souls

I had overcome her powers, proving myself stronger than any mortal man. No one would question my loyalty to the King, or to God, after enduring and passing this test of faith. These thoughts drove me forward through the deep shadows of the forest.

A wolf calls in the distance
Its cry answered by another
…and another
The call of a pack
Approaching from all directions
Surrounded

They were close now, the Wulfhednar, the wolf warriors. The witch had sent them after me, even though she had promised to let me go. It was all a part of her game, a ruse of deceit and broken promises.

Baiting me with lies
Her alluring body
The pleasures of her touch

Her skilled hands had cared for me, and on black wings, the Raven had carried me from death back to life. She had frustrated and enraged me, assaulting me with powers I had never fought before.

And I had almost succumbed to it all—to her.

Almost.

I forced my legs to move faster, welcoming the pain of the stones and barbed twigs that pierced my feet. It took my mind off things I did not want to ponder and feelings I did not want to suffer.

I had left behind my wolf skin, my birth name, Gerwulf, and my identity as a Wulfhedinn. I dared not believe she would never truly release me.

She follows
Soaring above as the Raven
Covering me with shadow
Calling

I hunger
Feed me, Wulfhedinn

As the Walkyrie, she had marked me as one of her Wulf-hednar, mixing my blood with theirs and hers. She would try to draw me back to don the wolf skin and to invoke the demon again. I gritted my teeth and squared my shoulders. No, the Eater of Souls would no longer feast on my sin.

As I ran, anger replaced fear, and I pushed myself harder. Sweat poured from my body, and my lungs wheezed for more air. Would her pack of wolf beasts tear me apart or drag me back to the stone tower? I would never know, because they would not catch me.

I darted through the trees, but soon they grew so thick I had to squeeze between them in many places. The soaring branches blocked the sun, leaving me nothing with which to guide my course. The entire forest floor was in shadow, and every bough and trunk looked the same. Had I passed this way before?

I sniffed, hoping to detect a stream in which I could drown my scent and confuse the pack of Wulfhednar, but there was none. I searched for a break in the foliage that might indicate an open meadow, but shadow and darkness ruled the bewitched

Teutoburg Forest. I ran several more miles before I stumbled and fell. Gasping, trying to rise, my head spinning, my legs collapsed under me. I sniffed and did not sense the wolf demons. I had lost them and could rest, just for a moment.

I lay there, panting. Had it all been a nightmare? The Raven, the tower prison, the Wulfhednar—they were conjured by the witch, with her potions that poisoned my mind. Wulfhednar were simply men who wore wolf skins, and I could outrun men. Yes, I could outrun mere mortals.

Bounding through the brush
Drawing closer
They howl
Signaling attack

One leaps from the mist
Fangs bared, lips curling
Snapping, biting
Tearing at me
…gone

Snarling from behind
Another one jumps
Hungry breath in my face
Ripping my throat
…gone

Blood pours
Choking on it
Drowning
Warm on my shredded skin

They howl
Behind me
In front of me
Calling to one another
Ringing in my ears
Surrounded

Gasping, heart thumping, I rolled on the ground and grasped at my neck, but it was intact and unbloodied. I jumped to my feet, finding my body whole and unharmed. Which direction had they come from? I ran before I could think more about it. I could not stay still, inviting another attack, real or imagined.

The howling fades
Farther behind with every step

…quiet
Too quiet

I stopped, cupping my ears to sharpen my hearing. The silence turned my sweat-covered body to ice. I tried to convince myself again they were merely men—and failed.

Wulfhednar—I could not lose them so easily.

They would stalk silently now, in a hunt for prey, waiting for the crucial time for their ambush. Whether real or conjured by the witch, they could rip out my throat if they chose.

I had to get to the safety of the King's road, which marked the border of the Christian lands. King Karl's soldiers patrolled there, protecting Christians from the Saxon rebels, and God watched over it, keeping the pagan demons at bay. It could not be far now.

My throat was dry and tight from thirst, and blood seeped from my slashed feet. I remembered the enchanted swamp and its deadly sedges. They and the Teutoburg Forest surrounded and protected the Raven's Stones where the witch had imprisoned me.

Mist swirls
Veiling giant pillars of white stone
They emerge from vapor
Towering above me in the moonlight
Silvery gods rising

The Raven soars
You have come to my stones, Wulfhedinn

Attacked and beaten
Tied and bound
Held captive in the tallest stone

The fog rises again
Surrounding me
In cold rock and foreboding chill

I had to keep running.

The sedges of the swamp concealed a mire that could trap and drown a man who trod carelessly. I should have been testing the ground before every footfall. I should have been watching for growths of vines that moved like snakes and hawthorn thickets with thorns that could impale me, but I was fleeing too fast for caution.

I considered stopping to pray, to beseech God for His guidance through the witch's forest and her swamp. I wanted to hold my cross, but it had been lost it to the witch. God would not hear my prayers without it—not in the depths of the pagan wilds. I was on my own, alone.

One foot sank slightly into spongy ground. Before I could stop, my next step broke through a thin layer of dirt between the roots of a tree. I dropped to my hips into cold muck and water. Grabbing an overhanging branch, I pulled myself out, finding footing on a large tree root. I broke off a piece of the branch and poked the ground before me, testing each step.

My pace slowed to that of a slug. Moving so deliberately, I was an easy target. I weighed the risk of a cautious pace versus breaking into a run. My instinct was to flee, but my thoughts focused on the danger of drowning in the swamp. I continued to test every step until I saw a small break in the dense foliage. The spot was close, a mere twenty paces away. As I neared, a path emerged. There was a slice of open sky above it, and I could see the sun. It had not risen yet to midday, throwing shadows that pointed west, giving me bearings.

The path was not well worn, but it was distinct enough to follow. It led southwest, in the direction of the Hellweg, the King's road. The road would take me to the Frankish garrison and Paderborn, where King Karl's palace overlooked the great walled town. The path was hard and dry, so I dropped the stick and hastened my pace.

A breeze blew down the narrow opening in the foliage, carrying the scent of smoke. I was close to a village. Soon the smoke thickened, heavy with char. It did not smell like a cooking fire, blacksmith's forge, or soldier's campfire; something had been put to the torch.

I came to the edge of smoldering fields. They surrounded the remains of burned-out cottages and a feasting hall. I knew the place, once a prosperous Saxon hamlet. Now most of the buildings had collapsed into debris. A few charred walls remained standing, threatening to topple. The church was the only intact structure.

The people of this village had sworn oaths of loyalty to King Karl, but in secret they had plotted rebellion. They had accepted baptism as Christians, while slipping into the forest to worship the old gods. They had kept their secrets safe until I overheard their conspiracy and reported it. I had done my job well as the King's Royal Scout and Huntsman.

I smelled something else, the stink of putrid flesh. A dark mass dangled from a tree on the opposite side of the fields. I ducked low and moved closer until I saw it clearly—a man hanging by the neck. His head was tilted to the side unnaturally, the face hidden in shadow. The breeze blew past me and turned his limp body and swollen gray face into the sunshine. The village elder.

Another body hung in the next tree—smaller, thinner, and beardless. The elder's defiant son. He had been impatient to rebel against the Frankish king, wanting to die as a warrior to prove his courage to Wodan. Instead, he dangled in the air as a traitor.

More bodies with bloated gray faces hung nearby. I counted five more men and a dozen women and children.

Wars should be fought among grown men, I thought, but changed my mind. The Saxon women of this village had favored rebellion as much as the men and had been ready to take up arms. They had known they were breaking the King's law—and the punishment for it. They had chosen their fate.

I wanted to believe that, but my spying on them had ensured their deaths, and they had died as prisoners with their hands bound behind them.

The wind changed direction, carrying a heavy gust of smoke. Ashes flew into my eyes and soot choked my throat. I coughed, sure I would hear the Raven, the shriek of the Eater of Souls calling for me.

Like ice on my neck
Like death on my shoulder

The Raven
Perches on the hangman's tree
Screeching
Her beak dripping blood

Feed the wolf
Feed the Raven

I bolted from that cursed place. It was about three miles from the farthest reach of the King's road and the safety of the Lippespringe garrison. I would be there soon.

I ran through midday and afternoon, but I got no closer to the road and no farther from the contorted faces of the hanging corpses. The images did not fade until late in the day, when shadows lengthened and the temperature cooled. Dusk crept into the woodland, and the forest floor grew dark.

I kept running. I should have been there hours ago. I should have recognized something, but nothing was familiar. I covered more miles, listening for the sounds of an army garrison. I sniffed the wind for the scents of horses and men, but there was no hint I was getting closer. The forest grew thicker, and I had to slow my pace in the darkness.

My head was spinning, and fatigue was making it difficult to focus. Had I passed this way before? My movements were becoming awkward. My lungs burned, and my chest pounded. I fought to move forward and overcome the need for water, food, and rest.

I stumbled and collapsed, needing my last bit of energy to gasp for air. Curling into a ball, I rolled onto my side.

A swarm of black gnats rose in the cooling air. They covered my naked body and flew into my nose and mouth. I choked, defenseless against the smallest creatures without the wolf skin on my back and my axes in hand. I had left them behind with the witch, the Eater of Souls, high in the stone tower where she had held me.

I had to get up, keep going, and return to the service of King Karl. I had to retake my place with him. I had earned my position by returning the stolen Holy Spear, the King's precious and powerful holy relic. He had rewarded me richly, transforming me from a cursed beast into a Christian courtier.

Never to don wolf skin
Nor call upon the demon

I had not looked back at the witch when I made my escape. Her presence loomed above, tempting me to glance at her long black hair. I had felt her beguiling eyes watching as I ran down the winding stairway hewn into the huge stone, keeping my sights on my target—the freedom of the forest. I had slipped safely into the cover of the trees, the Raven shrieking after me.

Rocking on my side, I put my hands over my ears, but I could not block the sound of the Raven's call. Squeezing my eyes shut did not erase the image of the black scavenger perching over the hanged Saxons.

Another burden you cannot endure
The Eater of Your Soul

Water was flowing nearby. A shallow stream next to me trickled over rocks like the tears running down my cheeks. The gentle light of dawn danced on the clear little ripples. Had I slept—or had I cried—through the night?

My mouth ached from thirst, and I drank, cooling my parched throat. I spat grit and gnats from my teeth. Drinking again, I stared at my reflection in the water. My eyes were dark. The witch had said they were dark when I was angry.

My jaw was misshapen from the beating the Wulfhednar had given me nearly two months before. My beard and hair were wild and tangled. In my reflection, I looked for Tracker, the King's courtier, but all I could see was Gerwulf, the savage animal.

Neither Saxon nor Frank
Neither Christian nor pagan
Both man and beast

A lone wolf
Wulfhedinn

I panicked, fearing I might never find my way back to King Karl to reclaim my place as the King's man. I lurched away from the stream and scanned the sky for the Raven. It was clear and blue, unmarred by her black silhouette. She and the Wulfhednar provoked fear in me, and I despised it. I loathed the way they had forced me to flee recklessly like a defenseless fawn from hungry wolves. Rage shot through me like the venom of an angry wasp.

"You cannot keep me from my King and my God!" I shouted. "I will return and I will never fear you again."

The effort drained me, and I crumpled on the bank, letting my cheek rest in the cool water. "I am a Christian man," I whispered between gasps. "A Christian."

My thumping heart slowed, bones resting, and I drifted.

A Man with No Coin

Floating
A leaf on water
Slumbering in gentle waves
Something brushes the hair from my face
Fingers of a soft morning breeze
Caring for my broken body
Cradles my head in her arms

A woman's smell, one I knew.

"You have returned," she said.

The witch.

She poked me several times with a sharp stick. I groaned and jumped. My head was whirling, and I fell into the stream with a splash.

"It is about time," she said, jabbing me. "Get up."

I grabbed the stick and pulled her onto the muddy stream-bank. She was weak, not strong like the witch.

"You filthy lout!" she said, trying to wipe the grime from her face and clothing. "I have no other mantle. You ruined it."

My cheek tingled from her scratches. "You should not go poking men with sticks," I said.

"I thought you were dead," she said. "I almost sent for the body collector to haul you to the pit before you began to stink, but you stink already. It would serve you right to get thrown into it."

I ignored her, seeing a familiar timber wall behind her. The palisade of Paderborn. So, I had not run back to the Raven's Stones. I had found my way back to King Karl's palace and was safe within the Christian realm.

A cluster of cottages was nestled in the shadow of the wall. I knew these cottages, the brothel the King retained for his courtiers and high-ranking soldiers. I had forgotten my encounter there—until now.

She had knelt in front of me, unbuckled my belt, and pulled down my breeches. Blood rushed to my face. I was blushing.

"Do not ogle me like a dog sniffing after a bitch in heat," the whore said. "You never came back after the first time, and it is obvious now you are carrying no silver."

She made me mindful of my dripping nakedness. I stepped back, covering my loins with my hands, and slipped on a wet rock. I nearly fell, spreading my arms to catch my balance. I recovered myself and stepped carefully out of the stream.

"I have been scouting for the King," I said, my cheeks burning.

She laughed harshly. "You do not look like a Royal Scout now." Her sardonic tone was unlike the girl-child voice I remembered. The lines on her face were deeper, and her wide eyes were narrowed with suspicion.

"I need to see King Karl. Is he in Paderborn?" I asked impatiently. My gaze fell on her breasts, and I quickly looked away.

She frowned. "No. They say he is campaigning somewhere far to the west; the Spanish March they call it."

"Is General Theoderic here?"

"Yes, with his Scola soldiers. *They* often visit me—with their purses."

"And Brother Pyttel?"

"The King's monk?" She scoffed. "Who knows? He does not come here. A strange one he is. They say he spends his time alone in the woods, probably giving himself calluses and asking God to bless them." She sniggered, understanding the mad monk better than she knew.

"Yes, a very *pious* man of God," I said, thinking of the sacrilegious pagan sacrifice he performed at the pagan spring. I thought I had been the only one who knew. "I must get inside the palace and see the General."

"It will not be difficult for you, the great man who returned the Holy Spear to the King," she said. "The soldiers are quite jealous, but they will surely open the gates for you immediately—even without your breeches."

"I need clothing."

"You expect much for a man with no coin purse," she said, throwing her muddy mantle over my shoulders.

I smelled her body as she fussed with the wool, trying to arrange it so it covered both my front and backside. It was too short.

She chuckled. "That will not do."

She tied it around my waist, her hands brushing my belly wound. I flinched.

"How did you ever survive such an injury?" she asked.

"By God's grace." I secured the mantle myself, glad my belly and cullions were now covered from her probing eyes.

"Some said you had deserted," she said. "Others said you were killed, and they were nearly right."

She moved closer and pulled the loose material between my legs toward my waist. Her hands brushed my cock, cradling my balls for a moment. "Bring me some of the King's silver," she whispered, "and I will lick the pain and sweat off you."

Heat rushed between my legs. She smiled and leaned close to my bare chest.

"I can still smell the beast in you," she said.

I pulled away, tucking the mantle into my waist to create makeshift breeches. "I must go." I leaped past her, taking the path from the brothel to the Hellweg.

"You owe me a new cloak," she called after me.

King Karl's road was deeply rutted with cart tracks. The footprints of his infantry and the horseshoes of his heavy war-horses had also left their mark. Soldiers stood guard along the road, keeping a sharp eye on all those who approached Pader-born and the King's palace inside its walls.

From the northeast, Saxon peasants led half a dozen oxen teams toward the gate. Their carts were loaded with grain and barrels of beer. They appeared compliant with the King's order to provide him and his army with goods. Some of these peasants might be rebels, or maybe not. I could not tell. If the King continued to press them with high church taxes and more demands, any of them might turn and fight for the rebel leader Widukind. Already they were required to deliver large amounts of livestock, leather, grain, beer, and labor.

The Saxon peasants prodded the oxen teams with sticks, leading them by lines tied to large nose rings. The oxen trudged forward—all but the largest one. It stopped abruptly, snorted, and threw its head. The nose ring tore, and blood dripped. The driver cursed and beat the ox, but it refused to move. He beat it harder and whipped its nose until it relented. The wooden wheels of the cart creaked slowly past me.

I am not a chained beast
No longer

The gate opened for the Saxon ox train. The ripe smell of manure and human waste wafted out, and I covered my nose. The towering timber wall of Paderborn might keep out the rebel heathens, but it sealed in a mass of people and animals and their vile stink. I had almost forgotten the oppressive confines of the town. The witch had walled me in too, caging me in her stone chamber. She had controlled my will with potions and poisons like the King controlled the Saxons with taxes.

Panic surged through my veins, as if Wulfhednar were still on my trail. I dodged into the shelter of the trees, suddenly preferring to face them than a city of Christians. The fresh air of the wilds called with the voice of blowing grasses and rustling leaves. I wanted to run far away. I had escaped the tiny prison where the witch had held me, so why did entering a large town of God-fearing Christians feel so daunting? I took a step forward and could go no further. I needed help. I needed God.

I pulled a loose strand of wool from the mantle and wrapped it around two twigs to fashion a primitive cross. Finding strength in both the task and the cross, I clutched it between folded hands and knelt.

"Holy Father in Heaven. Thank you for the strength and courage to defy the pagan demons. Be with me as I return to the Christian realm."

I waited for a sign God had accepted my prayer, but the forest remained quiet—no different than before I had prayed. My mother had told me I had been blessed by both gods, Wodan the Saxon war god and the Christian God, but now I was as alone as I had been while caged in the stone tower.

I flung the cross. Why did God refuse to touch me with His grace? The familiar answer came to me from a memory, a voice of madness and reason. Brother Pyttel.

Give it time
Stop brooding

Fight for God
Fight for your soul

When all was in despair, the monk's words had helped sustain me, and now they helped me to see I was facing yet another trial from God. I reclaimed the cross and tied it around my neck. Nothing could be more difficult than what I had suffered the last couple of months. I would pass this test. I would conquer it.

Pushing aside some branches, I peered at the palisade gate. Sentries in mail armor were questioning the Saxon ox drivers and examining their goods. The soldiers looked so strong in their coats of heavy cold rings. I would wear that armor again soon.

Before I could stop myself, I thought of my soft, warm wolf skin. It had shielded me for so long, as well as armor, but I refused to yearn for it. Let it rot in the stone tower.

I returned to the road and approached the gate, unsure if the guards would arrest or welcome me. It had been months since I had been at Paderborn, and few people had seen me closely. Now, I looked like I did when I first came to the King's town, like an animal from the wilds, but I was no longer that beast. I had redeemed my soul and earned my place here, as Brother Pyttel had said. I had conquered death and defied the witch and the wolf demons. I had proven myself to the King and to God. I had every right to enter the town and the King's palace and reclaim what was mine.

The guards finished searching the Saxons' carts. They waved them through the gate and raised their spears as I neared.

I pushed the hair out of my face and tucked it behind my ears. Setting my jaw, I held my head high. The guards gawked at me, and one of them called the captain.

"By God's grace, a scout has returned from the forest!"

"It is the *Royal* Scout," said another, his mouth dropping.

The captain of the guard approached, squinting at me. "Finally," he said, "some good news for the General."

He escorted me through the town toward the palace. The narrow streets were crowded with people, chickens, dogs, pigs, and goats. Church bells rang the hour, deep and lonely, shaking my bones.

Bong, bong, bong.

Horses whinnied, and blacksmiths' hammers pounded iron. Whack! Whack! Whack!

Everything was crowding me, sucking the air away. Sweat rolled down my forehead, and hair fell from behind my ears, covering my face. I gladly hid behind it. Why had I wanted to come here? My heart was pounding so hard, it was impossible to remember. I was reliving a nightmare, walking through the crowd as a spurned and beaten animal. I clenched my fists, the only weapons I had left.

Eyes ogled me from every window and alleyway. Voices called out from street to street. There was so much shouting I could not hear it all the voices at once, so I listened to one at a time.

"It is Tracker!"

"The Royal Scout!"

"He has returned!"

I peeked through my tangled hair and saw smiling faces. People were waving and cheering, welcoming me. I did not know how to respond, but it was not a time to fight, so I raised my head and dropped my fists.

The Looking Glass

I was taken to my old quarters next to General Theoderic's. The room was undisturbed, as I had left it. It was strange he had not given it to anyone else while I had been gone. Many would have coveted their own room.

"Some refreshments for you until dinner." The groom gestured to the servants bringing beer, bread, and cheese. He rubbed his nose as he scanned me from head to toe. "We will draw you a bath, and fresh clothes are in order as well." He clapped his hands at the servants, and several jumped to his bidding.

"General Theoderic will be returning to the palace for dinner," he said. "He will be anxious to see you, and we must have you ready for an audience with him."

I tried to run my fingers through my tangled beard. "I will shave myself," I said.

"As you wish."

They left me alone as I devoured the bread and cheese, washing it down with the entire flagon of beer. Belching, I anticipated a soothing bath in a steaming tub. I wanted to scrub away everything that had happened from the last months, the last years—my entire life. A shave and new breeches would banish it all for good.

Free me
From the Raven
The witch
The Walkyrie
…the woman

Servants brought far more food than I could eat, as if they were afraid to let me go hungry. I ate and drank until my stomach ached and my head spun. Belching, I pushed clumps of hair out of my eyes. Much of my meal had landed in my beard. I tried to brush off the bread crumbs and pieces of cheese. Filling another cup of beer, I saw the shiny object nearby on the table—a looking glass.

It glistened, calling me to peek at it. I pushed it farther away and drank. The silvery surface continued to entice me, temping me until I covered it with the breadbasket.

The servants dragged in a copper tub and filled it with steaming water. They left me a razor and comb but did not stay to assist me. I was sure they remembered the last time they tried to groom me. They would not want to repeat that encounter and wisely left me to do it myself.

I bathed quickly, afraid soaking too long in the hot water might soften my muscles and weaken my mind. I was unsure how the uncompromising General would receive me. He clearly had left orders to see to my comfort, but he would still question me fiercely. I needed to keep my thoughts sharp.

I hacked through the beard with shears, most of it falling on the floor in clumps. I left enough on my face to fashion a long drooping moustache, one of the marks of Frankish nobility. I ran my finger along the iron razor blade, shining without a trace of rust. It had a bronze handle in the shape of a wolf. Had it been made just for me?

I shaved as best I could without using the looking glass. Blood dripped down my face and neck from nicks the razor made. Stinging, the little cuts were causing far more pain than they should.

She kisses the blood away
She kisses the pain away
Stroking my battered jaw

You are not as strong as you believe, Wulfhedinn

Her lips on mine, her mouth covering mine
Devours me
With her lies
Her deceptions

I flung the razor with its wolf-head handle. "I am stronger than you, witch."

The razor nearly hit the groom as he opened the door. His eyes bulged, and he dove back behind the door, slamming it shut.

"Lord Huntsman." His voice was muffled behind the timbered door. "The General is in his quarters and will see you now."

By Blood and by Will

General Theoderic peered over his cup of beer. His icy gaze was cunning and unreadable. The deep scars on his bald head spoke more than he ever did—as did his choice to drink beer and not spend extra money on wine. He had not changed.

"So at least one of my scouts has returned alive," he said gruffly, but the corners of his lips lifted subtly. It hinted of a grin, a rare expression for him. I pretended not to see it, but he knew I noticed. Nothing escaped him.

"The monk will be glad to see you," he said. "The King sent Brother Pyttel beyond the Teutoburg Forest to Eastphalia, Saxony. He has been overseeing the building of churches and baptizing the Saxons there. They appear to be more receptive to Christianity than their cousins in Westphalia. Anyway, the monk is due back within a fortnight to bless the next section of the King's road."

It was good to hear news of Pyttel. I hoped he would survive his journey through Eastphalia. Some of the Eastphalian Saxons, who had been loyal to the King, had now been recruited as rebels—news I was not eager to tell the General.

The General stood and gestured toward a stool. "Sit, Royal Scout and Huntsman." He paced, his hands clamped behind his back. "I will either reward you for returning or hang you for desertion."

Desertion?

"I am no deserter," I snapped.

"Any time one of my men vanishes, I presume he is a deserter until proven otherwise," he said. "After your disappearance, I sent other scouts to track you."

"I was captured by Saxon rebels," I said. "Your scouts would never have found the place where they took me."

"And where was that?"

I resented his suspicious tone and refused to bow to it. I had survived the Wulfhednar and was not afraid of him.

"You threatened to hang me," I said. "Why should I tell you anything? You will likely call me a liar. I might as well make my own noose."

"It is your duty to report everything you know," he said. "You are the only scout I have sent into the Teutoburg Forest who has returned. The bodies of the others have been found decapitated and mauled—"

"As if attacked by the Wulfhednar?"

He scowled. "Demon wolf warriors—humph."

I met his steely eyes and pulled off my tunic. He glanced over the scars on my arm and leg and blinked several times at the hole in my abdomen. It had startled him, and he tried to hide it.

"This is what the Wulfhednar can do to a man," I said. "I was attacked and taken prisoner by Widukind's band of Wulfhednar." I put the tunic back on. "Judge me, as you will."

"You deserted nearly two months ago on Hexennacht, Witches' Night," he continued as if unmoved by what he had seen. "You should have been locked in a church that night, praying for God's protection from the magic of the so-called demons and witches, like the rest of us."

"*You* sent me out on patrol, but I would have gone into the woods whether you ordered me or not," I said. "I could not do my job hiding in a church, especially on Witches' Night."

"Indeed." His tone grew sharp. "What did these fiendish rebels do with you for so long?"

"Held me in a stone tower."

"A stone tower? I have not seen anything but timber hillforts and mud huts in Saxony, although some have foundations of stone."

"It was not a hillfort or a fortress built by men. I was held at the Raven's Stones."

He cocked his head. "The Externsteine?"

"Yes, in a chamber at the top of the tallest pillar."

He cracked his knuckles, one at a time. "Why would heathen devils capture a Christian and keep him alive in their sacred place?"

"I do not know."

"They wanted something from you, or they would have butchered you, like they have my other scouts."

"I do not know," I repeated.

He stood and leaned close to me. "You are lying." His breath was hot on my neck, and I could almost feel the blue vein throbbing in his temple. "You cannot hide the truth from me. I know what you are—that monstrosity, the bastard of a Christian whore and Saxon Wulfhedinn."

I jumped, knocking the stool over.

Fangs bared
Tear into his Christian face

I hunger
Feed me, Wulfhedinn

I threw a punch at him. He pulled away so fast my fist barely grazed his cheek. He did not raise a hand to return the blow or draw a weapon on me. I waited for him to call his guard to arrest me, but he stared at me with his icy eyes.

He had always known what I was.

The wolf fades
Gone into darkness

"It is obvious what they want," he said. "They want you for their rebel army of Wulfhednar."

I avoided his gaze.

"Why did you not stay with them?" he asked. "You are as much a pagan as you are a Christian."

"I am *no longer* Wulfhedinn," I said. "While I was captured, every thought I had was fixed on returning to my King. When I had healed and regained my strength, I escaped and left the wolf skin behind."

"You only returned here to claim title and riches from King Karl," he said. "Those barbarians could not match what he offers you, could they?"

"I return to my King and my God, the God I was raised with, the faith in which my mother baptized me."

He tore my primitive cross off my neck and flung it to the floor. "Do you think you could fool me with two sticks strung together? Where are your real cross and the jeweled sword the King gave you?"

I flashed him a defiant glare. I had not tried to hide the fact I had lost them. It would have been a weak gesture, and he would have eventually noticed they were gone. Let him see I no longer had them, so the reason for their loss would stand all the stronger.

"She took them," I said.

"She?"

"—the witch."

Eater of Souls
Blood-stained beak
Drinking her fill
Never quenched
Never satisfied

He grunted. "The witch they say protects the Externsteine and the Wulfhedinn warriors with magic?"

"She is called the Walkyrie by the Saxons," I said.

"Walkyrie." He scoffed. "The peasants are terrified that no Christian man can overcome her powers. What truth to this?"

"She has no power over me—none of them do."

The General's lips remained tight, his face like stone.

"They had the power to capture and hold you for weeks," he said.

"And yet, I returned."

He harrumphed. "So, what can you tell me about Widukind?" he asked.

"He and his wolf warriors were there at the Raven's Stones. I saw them worshiping Wodan and invoke wolf demons with a ritual of fire and blood—" The scar on my chest was burning. I rubbed it, but it continued to smolder under my skin like a glowing coal.

Spilling and mixing our blood together
She cuts us all
Binds us all
The Wulfhednar, the Walkyrie
And me

"How many Wulfhednar are there?" he asked.

"A dozen."

"Only twelve." He tapped his fingers on the table. "So, the rumors Widukind is raising a *large* army of Wulfhednar are untrue."

"He is also training Saxon freemen and half-free to fight."

"A handful of rustics with kitchen knives and farm tools?"

"Many more."

He raised an eyebrow nearly imperceptibly. "How many?"

"Thousands. More come every day."

The General's lips parted slightly. "Can you count so great a number?"

I glared at him. "They are coming from all over Saxony, beyond Widukind's own Westphalian tribes. The Wulfhednar are training them to fight with bows and the Saxon long daggers—the seaxes. Some are armed with swords."

"Swords?" he asked. "To have such resources, they must be supported by more nobles than we expected. Did they train on horseback as well?"

"Some."

"Was Count Sidag there?"

"I am not sure. From the top of the tower I could not see the faces of the rebels clearly—except the witch."

"Can you identify this woman?"

I hesitated.

You are bound to me, to the pack
By blood and by will
—if it be your will

Fight for your soul

"Yes," I said.

"Good. Rumors of this witch and her warriors have spread like the pox from the peasant class, to the freemen, to the nobility. It is causing fear and doubt in my most hardened Scola horsemen. They must not learn of the truth of these rumors, or it could cripple my army. You will not speak of it to anyone, even the monk. Tell people you have spent the last months scouting, but do not offer any more information."

"Understood," I said.

We talked into the night. He asked for more details about the rebels: how they trained, the tactics they were using, and their morale. His hard expression did not change as I described how their recruits arrived at the Raven's Stones as simple peasants and left as proficient warriors, trained by Widukind and his Wulfhednar.

"They have no intention of submitting to King Karl or to the Lord God," I said. "And mark my words. They will take bloody vengeance tenfold for the Saxon men, women, and children your soldiers hung from trees."

Theoderic lifted his chin, deepening the rolls on the back of his neck.

"I saw them on my way back from the Raven's Stones," I said.

"Yes, the traitor village," he said. "By all appearances, they *were* honoring their baptism and their oaths to the King. Your spying brought their true nature to light, but not one of them would reveal the location of Widukind and his Wulfhednar, even as they watched their children hang."

The General's eyes burned into mine as I tried to erase the image of their contorted gray faces, nooses tight around their necks. I fought to hold his gaze without squirming.

"A Wulfhedinn raped your mother, did he not?" he asked slowly, deliberately.

I could not answer him, trying to forget what the witch had told me about her.

Your mother loved the Saxon Wulfhedinn
And he loved her
Life would have been worse for you both had the truth been
known

Here, behind stout palisade walls, she was again trying to poison my mind. My mother could not have loved a Wulfhedinn. No. Never.

"A Wulfhedinn took my mother, and created me—an aberration who was damned by God," I said. "I despise him and all Wulfhednar like no others."

The General tilted his head, examining me closely. "Good," he said. "Hanging those traitors in the Saxon village should lure the fiends from their dark holes. In the light of day, you and my Scola riders should be able to quickly cut them down. The King has a storehouse full of wolf skins outside the palace. Go there and pick one that calls out the dark magic and power of the Wulfhedinn."

"This is all I need," I said, retrieving my cross and tying it around my neck. "I will fight like any other Christian Frankish soldier, under God."

"The King did not make you his Royal Scout and Huntsman for your piety."

His blunt words struck me hard. I had been tested and had proven my piety twice over, earning my redemption and my place as a Christian soldier.

"I will fight better with God at my side than with a wolf in my heart," I said. I would prove it to him, to the King, and to myself.

"As you wish, Tracker." He turned his back and took a small sip from his cup. "But I fight warriors, not demons and magic—that is your task, Wulfhedinn."

Rutting Pig Noises

I returned to my room. Servants had lit tallow candles in my absence. The General must have ordered the luxury, a quiet gesture of great favor from him. He himself worked by the light of oil lamps although he could afford candles. I smirked. He had no intention of hanging me for desertion—not if he thought me useful.

What would he have me do? Send me in pursuit of Widukind? But he would not risk it without a well-armed force to back me, and it would be impossible to get a force large enough through the thick Teutoburg Forest without a road. He likely would keep me closer, patrolling, until the road was complete.

The acrid odor of smoking animal fat from the candles was stinging my nose. A luxury, yes. But I preferred the smell of wood smoke from an open fire. I blew out the candles and opened the shutters. Fresh air blew in, and moonlight fell across the stone floor. Light streamed from the General's window next to mine. I smelled an oil lamp.

Our meeting was keeping him awake. I pictured his cold eyes squinting over maps as he adjusted his plans for the Hellweg based on what I had told him. He would scratch his scarred bald head, trying to word a message to the King in the best way. I had not brought good news about the rebellion, but the information was invaluable to him and the King, more than he admitted.

Maybe all I had suffered at the hands of the witch had been worthwhile. Still, I had no weapons and would not be of much use to the General without them. When would he provide them, and what they would be? I was better with an axe than a sword, but I wanted a sword, the blade of a titled soldier of the King. Axes were for barbarians.

I sat on the wide windowsill, my throbbing feet and tired legs dangling over the courtyard. I felt weightless, as if I could almost fly. Like the Raven.

Frowning, I scanned the sky for her. Would she dare fly into the courtyard of King Karl's palace? I slipped back inside and closed the shutters.

Exhausted, I undressed and fell into bed. The wool-stuffed mattress was raised off the floor away from drafts, unlike the hard pallets I had slept on. Sinking into the soft mattress, I tossed and turned, and my mind refused to rest.

I assumed the General would have me scout the route for the Hellweg, but I wanted him to send me far away. I longed to go to the other side of the Frankish kingdom, far from the witch and the Wulfhednar. The General would keep me near though. Finishing the road was a critical strategy in his war against the Saxons. It would allow the army to march into the heart of rebel territory, the Teutoburg Forest and the Raven's Stones, where I never wanted to return.

Maybe the King would send for me once he heard I had re-turned. I remembered how he drank deeply and laughed heart-ily. He had promised a hunting outing in the fall. I imagined us riding together at full speed through a forest rich with deer and boar. It was a woodland far from here, the kind of place of great dreams, which I would not have that night. I could not sleep.

I rose, wrapped myself in the whore's mantle, and lay on the stone floor. I was used to a harsher bed. It made it easier to ac-cept a harsh reality. The King would not take me hunting soon; he would keep me here until every Saxon rebel was killed.

Finally, I dozed until awakened by a flickering light. Some-one was in my room—a hooded figure holding a rushlight.

I jumped, startling the intruder. His hood fell back, reveal-ing a crushed nose, crooked brow, and tonsured hair in disarray. He smelled of putrid goat's blood.

Brother Pyttel.

His mouth dropped, the color draining from his face. "A ghost!" He touched my shoulder and patted the length of my arm. "Yes, you are real, but you look like a badger who lost a fight with a bear. You stink like one too. Are you dying?"

"I am not going to die."

He lowered the rushlight and examined my stomach. I wrapped the mantle around me, but it was too late. He had seen everything.

"God in Heaven!" he exclaimed. "Did someone tear out your bowels and slice off your limbs? And your face—" He gri-maced, twisting his scarred brow. "Horrible. But I knew you would return. God told me."

In the dim light, I glimpsed traces of dried blood at his hairline. He had performed blood sacrifice to the heathen gods again, probably while bathing at the pagan spring.

"At least you have washed," he said. "I cannot imagine what you smelled like before."

"No worse than you, Brother."

He embraced me tightly until my belly ached. I suppressed a groan and pulled away.

"What in the name of God and the Holy Spirit happened to you?" he asked. "There were so many rumors. Some said you had deserted. Others thought we would find your head staked on a pole like the other scouts—and where is your wolf cloak? I am usually the one prancing around naked in the dark." He chuckled.

I had not heard so much prattle in a long time; it was making my head ache. He was like the stinging hairs of a nettle plant. "I cannot give you answers if you do not shut your mouth," I said.

He put two fingers over his lips and nodded.

"I lost it," I said.

You cannot hide under the wolf's hide
From your deeds
From your God

The witch's words rung true. I would no longer shroud myself from God in the guise of the Wulfhedinn. At the same time, it nagged at me I might have done exactly as she intended.

Had I escaped her, or had she *let me go*?

I was glad Pyttel distracted me with another question.

"You *lost* it?" he asked.

The rushlight flame flickered and burned out, leaving us in darkness and silence. He had more questions tumbling through his mind; he always did.

"I will speak no more of it," I said, lying on the floor.

"Do you not remember any of the courtly courtesies I taught you, my friend?" he asked. "You failed to inquire about my state."

"How are you, monk?" I asked gruffly.

"Well, because you cannot contain your concern for me, I will tell you. My mission into Saxony was miserable, two months of baptizing the heathens in drenching rains. I hardly needed a river; they were soaked to the bone, and I fear their oaths washed away as quickly as the flooding streams." He groaned, rubbing his back. "How this old back aches from digging in the muddy ground. Such agonies I suffered in vain! Building churches while they continued to worship the old gods in oak tree groves. They likely burned the churches as soon as I left. I am no simpleton; I know they only cooperated because the Scola horsemen came with me. And they would have skinned me alive had I not sacrificed to Wodan with them."

I tried not to entertain his dubious reasons for his rites of sacrilege.

"I have seen you slit the throat of a man well enough," I said, rolling over on the floor. "They are probably afraid of you, you lunatic. You can have the bed, but I do not want to hear your rutting pig noises."

He cackled softly, and I shut my ears to his nighttime doings. Compared to what I had endured, tolerating the mad monk was like tolerating a fly on my face—irritating, but not too bad.

A Serious Defeat

In the morning, two servants brought us food and beer to break our fast. They bowed to Brother Pyttel. One of them fell to his knees, kissing the hem of the monk's habit.

"Praise God you have returned safely from the heathens," he said. "I must talk with you, Brother. I have waited so long. I have much to—"

"There will be time for confessions later," he said, waving him away. "Seek me out in two days' time in the chapel."

The servant bowed several times. "Thank you, Brother. Thank you."

"Try not to do anything that will double your penance between now and then," Pyttel said, shoving cheese into his mouth faster than he could possibly swallow it.

"Yes, Brother."

Pyttel sighed. "I will get no peace here in Paderborn. By noon, every sinner in the palace will be hanging on my habit, pleading for forgiveness, while planning to sin again. Some days, I wish I had never left the solitude of the monastery and become an ordained priest. I almost miss the vow of silence."

I choked on my beer. "*You* took a vow of silence?"

He blushed. "I admit I failed miserably at keeping it, but the abbot insisted it was necessary for me."

"Or for him."

He harrumphed, took a long swig of beer, and ate more cheese. "I do not miss monastery food, though. How I hate boiled fish and oats!" He grimaced. "I eat much better in the service of the King, but I tell you this—I have earned every bite of this fine white bread," he said, smearing a piece with butter. "The King expects too much of me, to act as a court scribe and to convert the entire pagan population in Saxony. As if it were so simple! And I constantly face a barrage of sinners needing confession."

"Give them harsher penances, and they will seek out other priests," I said.

He scratched his tousled tonsure and smiled under his crooked nose. "Yes, I am too soft and a poor judge of sin. I can condemn no one." He tilted his head, and his eyes sparkled. "Even a Wulfhedinn."

Pyttel had a talent for insulting me in a manner that lifted my dark spirits.

"It is good to see you smile and laugh," he said. "Something—or someone—must have given you practice in merriment these last couple of months."

Moonlight dances
Across her breasts
Shimmering
Over waves of long black hair

My mind drifted. I did not want to go back, to that day, that place, but I could not stop the journey once it had begun.

She laughs and splashes me
I am swimming toward her
She veers out of reach, giggling
Vanishing under the water
Her hands running up my thighs
Gripping my ass
Stroking my cock
Sliding her body against mine
Hair and eyelashes glisten with droplets
Wet lips meeting mine
Drinking the taste of her
Sweet musk and hawthorn

She lifts the goblet in a toast
Her poison burns my throat
Tainting my mind
Witch
Deceiver

The Raven shrieks
Standing before me
Alight by fire bolts
Her bloody beak and breasts drawing close
To devour me

Feed the wolf
Feed the Raven

The beast's beating heart steals inside me
Pounding harder and harder
A growl rises
Teeth bared
Snapping
Snarling
Rage and fury beyond bearing

Pyttel choked, spitting out the bread. "Wulfhedinn!" he cried between gasps.

The rage faded quickly. It always did when I was with the monk. "I am no longer Wulfhedinn."

He took a swig of beer to clear his throat and coughed several times. "Your demon eyes and snaggletooth snarl say different," he said. "How quickly you can snap! I missed your company these last two months, but I nearly forgot how I shit myself every time you incite the wolf. What brought it out? What were you thinking about?"

"I cannot talk about it," I said, adding, "by the General's orders."

"The General—bah!" He waved his hand dismissively. "I am your confessor, your link to God."

"I have no confessor."

"Well, it is high time you did. And who better than me? I have God's ear. Because of me, you have redeemed your sins. I saw the soul of the man inside the monster when no one else did. I brought you to the King, who gave you a title and an honored place in his court. Your trust in me did not come easy, but it has served you well."

His words tugged at me, drawing me reveal more. "I was captured and imprisoned by the Saxon rebels," I said. "On Hexennacht."

"God in Heaven, I thought as much. Where did they keep you?"

"In the Raven's Stones."

"The Raven's Stones? Inside those pillars of rock? How so?"

"There is a cell carved into the top of the tallest stone."

He scratched the bald spot on the top of his head. "How could you survive such a brutal beating in such a harsh place?"

"I survived. Nothing else matters."

He grabbed my arm and pushed up my sleeve. "Tell me about this wound—and all the rest. They must have been healed by someone skilled in the craft. Yes, I saw all your scars well enough last night—and that belly!" He shook his head and shuddered. "You would not have survived without a special healer who can wield the forces of life and death. Someone with magical powers and ties to the gods."

I pulled my arm away and pushed down the sleeve. "I laid in that dark place for a long time, with nothing but my faith in God to save me."

"Where, then, is your real cross?"

I shifted uncomfortably, pulling the tunic neckline over my handmade cross of twigs. I immediately regretted the feeble gesture to hide it. Why did I show such weakness to this mangled monk when I had stood so strong in front of General Theoderic?

He persisted. "Was it her, the Eater of Souls?"

I jumped from the table, knocking over the stool with a crash. "And where have *you* been all this time?" I retorted. "Emptying your cock into the Eye of Wodan at the pagan spring?"

He blushed and sighed. "Someone has to placate Wodan and the old gods in the old way, with pagan rite," he said. "God has told me this. It is the *only* way."

I snorted. The monk's mad cleverness had not changed while I had been gone.

He flashed a scowl at me and changed the subject. "So, the Eater of Souls saved your life, but she was not able to cage your spirit," he mused. "The Saxon peasants call her the Walkyrie, the Chooser of the Living and the Slain. They believe she holds the power of life and death and that she is the key to Widukind's rebellion."

"Peasants are fools." I did not sound convincing.

"Neither here nor there," he said. "The important thing is that you escaped her and returned here, to us, to God—a greater act of faith than any I have seen. God has taken note; you are highly favored, one of His most blessed. He has told me this. I want to hear the entire story, but now we need to talk of other matters."

"I have talked enough," I grumbled, pouring another cup of beer.

"You must listen," said Pyttel. "I have much to tell you before the General summons me into an endless interrogation about my mission in Saxony. That will be as delightful as lancing a carbuncle on my own ass."

He almost shoved the last piece of cheese in his mouth. Stopping himself, he offered it to me.

"Take it," I said, picturing the boil on his bare bottom and no longer hungry.

He shrugged and said, "The General dispatched a messenger as I arrived last night. He nearly trampled me at the gate, likely carrying news of your return to the King. The General has had no other good news for the King this summer. Has he told you about the road into the heathen forest?"

"No."

"I am not surprised. Theoderic is not a chatty hen, is he? He probably did not tell you his wife died either."

"He told me very little. Why would he tell me that?"

"Died of the bloody flux. God rest her soul. He also lost a son. Theoderic never speaks of him to anyone. In fact, we are all forbidden to discuss what happened, and I have said too much already, but to make my point—"

"Do you ever make your point, monk?"

"*Always*. Listen now. Theoderic's troubles with the Saxons and the road have grown worse every day since you disappeared. He must be glad to see you."

"Hardly. He threatened to hang me for desertion."

The monk cackled. "The crusty old fart had to save face. Then he sent you back to your noble quarters, indulging you with candles and a bed as soft as the King's." He fingered one of the extinguished wicks and flicked the ash. "He never meant to stretch your neck." He put his hand across his throat and make choking sounds, rolled his eyes back, and laughed.

I found no humor in it.

His face fell. "Just a little jest, my friend. You must learn to laugh more. It will help you make allies among the court—but not to worry about the General. His favor of you is high, I am sure. God has told me so." He winked. "And the Lord has *never* been wrong, but that is another matter. You must hear what I have learned from the guard at the gate. Guards see and hear everything. He said progress on the road came to a halt after you were captured, and I left on my mission. Heavy rains, nearly as epic as the biblical Great Flood, plagued the project. It poured until neither oxen, nor horses, nor men could free their legs from the mud. It took weeks to begin to dry out, and many areas are still an impassable swamp."

The monk gulped another cup of beer. "And there is more," he said. "Day after day, fewer Saxons reported to work on the project, breaking their oaths to provide labor for the King. The General sent Scola horsemen to round up the workers, but they could not find anyone. Entire Saxon villages had been abandoned. They had had taken everything with them, from cooking pots to livestock."

"They joined the rebellion," I said flatly.

Pyttel sighed in agreement. "I am afraid the King has lost them, and I have lost their souls to the old gods for good. The Scola riders destroyed their farms, and now they have nothing lose by staying with the rebellion. I must speak to the General about it today, but he barely tolerates my presence and will not listen to me. He may, however, listen to you."

"He knows what I am—what I *was*," I said.

The monk took another long drink of beer and belched deeply. "Ah. Not surprising. He is a cunning old fox, but he did not execute you. I would say he is glad to have a demon on his side."

"I am no longer a Wulfhedinn!"

"But can you separate the man from the wolf? Both can be ferocious—or not, so *use* the powers of both to do what is right." Pyttel set down his cup. "You have proven faith in God is stronger than all the powers of their pagan gods. Your defiance of the Wulfhednar and their witch is a victory for us and a serious defeat for the rebels."

It was a greater loss for them than the monk realized.

The drums pounding
Beating so hard
The echo of spirits ringing in my ears

From the pack, the largest Wulfhedinn steps forward
Speaking with the wolf's tongue

United with my son
My blood
Son of Widukind

No! I refused to accept it. I was not the rebel leader's son.

I expected more relentless questioning from the prying monk. Instead, he was looking vacantly at a spider crawling across the table. He mumbled to himself, drifting into lunacy. His babbling was too faint to hear at first, but it soon grew louder and clearer. "Oh yes, my Lord. In your great wisdom, you see it all." He snorted like a boar and smashed the spider under his hand. He popped it into his mouth, its legs still kicking, and swallowed with a contented smile.

"God has told me he approves of your cross of twigs," he said, licking his fingers. "He says it is better than a cross of silver or gold. He assures me it will help keep you strong as you learn to be patient. You will understand everything and see your path, in good time, in God's time."

"You have said that before," I grumbled. "When will it come to pass?"

"No one can tell you but your own soul," he said.

I had had enough of his mad prattling and was ready to snap at him, but before I could, he put a finger to my lips and shushed me.

"Think about this," he said. "You have mustered the strength to defy the powers of the Eater of Souls and her Wulfhednar— imagine what you can do with King Karl's army at your back."

Hero

Pyttel accompanied me through the long palace corridors, licking his lips in anticipation of dinner. How he could be so hungry after all he had eaten that morning?

"The General does not lay out a lavish feast like the King does," he said, "but it will probably be better than what the Saxons fed us."

She plies me with her magical stew
Deadening all pain
Crave her potion
Demand it
Knowing it weakens my resolve
Steals my will
Seduces me with her charms
Prisoner of her body
Drifting from meal to meal

Dream to dream
…captive

"The Saxons fed me poison," I muttered.

Pyttel raised a twisted eyebrow. I did not respond as the guards opened the heavy timber doors of the great hall. The doors creaked slowly on iron hinges, revealing a gloomy, cavernous room. I stopped in my tracks. We must have been in the wrong place.

Pyttel sighed. "The great hall is quite different when the King is not in residence and the General oversees the palace."

A weak light came from the open fire in the middle of the floor. It cast deep shadows across the huge stone walls like a fire in a cave. The last time I had been there, a thousand candles had thrown light into every corner of the King's feast.

Sparkling wine goblets
Rich tapestries
Bleached linen
Cushioned benches

The guest of honor
The savior of the stolen Holy Spear
Me

For the first time in my life, fortune had blessed me. While taking a piss in the brush, I had overheard the thieves and followed them to their hiding place. It had been easy to kill them and take the spear—and much harder to become the hero.

My trembling fingers had touched the spear tip that had pierced the Lord's ribs as he hung on the cross. His blood was alive on the tip—and full of power. The Raven had called to me, tempting me to run away with it and keep all to myself.

Feed the wolf
Feed the Raven

Defying their control over me, I had returned the spear to the King, its rightful master.

The King's servants had bathed and dressed me like a royal courtier, attempting to transform the frightful creature from the forest. They had cut my wild hair and had shaved my beard into a proper nobleman's moustache. It had not changed the savage wolf demon inside, damned by God and man alike.

The nobles of the King's court had envied, feared, and despised me. I had been an aberration, a curiosity, but I was a different man now. I had accomplished something few had ever done—a divine quest.

I held my head high, meeting the gaze of the crowd, as I walked to the General's table. He gestured toward an empty seat to his left. He did not stand to make a speech or tell a story to explain my absence the last two months. He acted as if I had not missed a meal there, as if nothing had happened.

Most of the other tables were packed with soldiers, the air of perfumed nobles replaced by an austere military presence. There were no candles and no glittering goblets. The stone walls and wooden tables and benches were bare, exactly how the General wanted them. My clenched jaw relaxed, and my tight shoulders dropped. I would manage easier with fighting men on wooden benches than courtiers on silk cushions.

I took a swig from my plain earthenware cup and tasted watered-down beer flavored with some bitter herb I did not recognize. It was so biting and difficult to swallow—so unlike like the rich, creamy beer the King had served. But I was grateful for it nonetheless.

Horse Master Gallo sat on the General's other side. He was second in command at the palace and had been sneering sideways at me ever since I walked in the door. He was not a man to hide his dislike of another, and his loathing of me was plain. Unlike the General, his opinions of people were easy to read in his manner. I respected that he could break and train a horse better than anyone in the kingdom, but I did not like him.

The Horse Master sucked his beer between missing teeth, making a loud slurping sound. Excess beer rolled down his face, dripping on his tunic. He acted as if he was unaware of it, but more likely, he did not care. I suspected he was trying to annoy the General. Pyttel had said Gallo was jealous of the General's higher position at court.

The table of the Scola horsemen was nearest our table. They did not wear their armor to dinner, but I identified them by their broad backs and hardened muscle. Each one wore a sheathed sword as a badge of noble prestige. It was unlikely they would need them for fighting while feasting safely inside the walls of Paderborn.

A handful of visiting nobles sat at the next table. They did not merit places ahead of the elite Scola horsemen. Some of the nobles were accompanied by wives and daughters, who softened the starkness of the military hall. I shifted in my seat to avoid looking at them, but my eyes wandered back to their table.

Gallo's daughter sat among them. She had his hooked nose and teeth that were too big for her mouth. She closed her lips, as if trying to hide them. She whispered to several other young girls, and they giggled, tossing their unbound hair.

Gallo harrumphed and slammed his cup so hard it rattled the spoons on the table. It startled everyone except the General. The girls quieted, blushing and trying to suppress more giggles.

Pyttel sat next to me, sniffed his beer cup and grimaced. "Not exactly the King's beer, is it?" he grumbled.

The General gave no sign he heard it, but he probably did.

Pyttel leaned toward me and whispered, "After the dreadful meeting I had with the General this afternoon, I would drink anything, even his beer."

More words of complaint were ready to roll off his tongue, but he was interrupted by a thumping sound. Soft and steady, the thumping grew louder and faster, echoing off the bare walls. The Scola riders had unsheathed their swords and were pounding the table with the pommels. Infantrymen used the butt end of daggers or seaxes, and the women joined in by clapping. The sound spread across the room in a rhythmic wave of booming applause.

I turned around to see who they were hailing, but there was no one behind me. The General had not made a speech, and he certainly would not have paid for minstrels, court poets, or acrobats to entertain his soldiers. What were they be applauding?

Brother Pyttel lifted his cup to me and said, "They are honoring you, Tracker. Word has spread fast of your captivity and return from the Saxons, and they have not forgotten your quest to return the Holy Spear." He winked. "You are still a hero. Soon the man, not the beast, will be legend."

Blood rushed to my face, and a warmth rose in my chest. It flowed from my heart through my body. The open fire flickered, the glow boosting the feeling. I had more than a place here; I was accepted and welcomed—by most.

The pounding faded as the servants brought in a meal of boiled meat and vegetables. The fare was simple compared to the King's feast of roasted meat, but it was hot and filling. There was no entertainment, but the soldier's voices were deep and robust, like the low rumbling of distant thunder when I was safely tucked in out of the rain. They laughed and teased one another, their merriment surrounding and embracing me like a fur mantle.

I was a part of it all now. I was one of them.

The General ate sparingly and did not comment on the applause, as if he expected no less. "You have not told me how you like your razor," he said.

I had almost forgotten the wolf-head razor. So, he *had* made it especially for me.

"It is—sharp," I said, running my hands across the small cuts on my neck. "Thank you."

"You will get better with it," he said dryly. It was almost a wry jest, and it put me to ease.

He cleared his throat. "Tomorrow we will go to the garrison at Lippespringe and survey the work completed on the road. I have ordered the armorer to supply you with weapons and armor." He leaned toward Horse Master Gallo. "Tomorrow morning, Horse Master, you will show the Royal Scout our best horses so he can pick a suitable mount."

Gallo grunted and opened his mouth. Large chunks of meat were caught in the spaces between his missing teeth. He let them fall from his mouth. He was mocking me.

The General did not acknowledge Gallo's behavior. "Good night, Horse Master." He rose from the table and nodded to me. "Royal Scout." He curled his upper lip at Pyttel and left.

"I do not have the favor of the General as you do," said Pyttel.

"My failed mission to Saxony has not helped my position. He interrogated me about it all afternoon." He shook his head, tapping his fingers on his beer cup. "It was not always this way. My past missions were fruitful, even after the King ordered the destruction of the Irminsul, their most sacred temple. They revered the Irminsul as the center of powerful magic—the great pillar that held up the skies."

The great pillar
Holding up the skies

I choked on my beer and slammed my cup. I knew these words, the words of the witch, the Walkyrie.

Today, on this longest of days
He descends the great stone pillar
He is healed
He is reborn
Gerwulf, son of Widukind

My mind had been reeling from her potion. Midsummer morning—I had climbed down the long staircase from the chamber, my prison at the top of the tallest of the Raven's Stones.

Pyttel rolled his crooked eyes. "Tracker, are you listening to me?"

"You talk too much," I said, wiping beer from my chin.

"I have to talk a lot so you will hear at least some of what I say," he said. "Anyway, it has been ten years since the King toppled the Irminsul at Eresburg. He is convinced he destroyed their gods and dark powers when their temple fell."

"He is wrong," I said. "The King did not destroy the only Irminsul. There is another—a stone pillar at the Raven's Stones. The Walkyrie who lives there has powers that are stronger and more frightening than anyone can imagine."

Pyttel shuttered. "I can imagine."

"Your sacrifices to their gods will no longer appease them," I said.

"Blast the King and his arrogance!" said Pyttel. "It is as if he wants to incite them with death threats and his outrageous taxes for worshipping the old gods. Now their anger has been compounded with Theoderic's order to hang their women and children—and this kind of incident is not the first one. It became clear during my miserable mission to Saxony that they will never forgive us for all these affronts. The King should have listened to me and allowed them to keep some traditions and rites. With time and compromise, the pagans would have slowly forgotten their old gods."

"It is too late now," I said.

He sighed in agreement. "I am afraid there is no alternative now but all-out war—a war that will benefit no one."

"A war their gods might win," I said.

The monk sunk his nose deeply into his cup. I indulged with him, wanting to forget everything about Saxons and rebels and war. The raucous laughter of the solders filled the hall. They laughed about simple things, everyday things, like the size of a comrade's nose or his cock. They taunted one another about falling from a horse or stumbling like a retching drunkard. I liked the soldiers' hall and the men in it.

The night grew late. Pyttel dropped his cup on the floor and almost fell off his stool.

"It is time for me to retire," he said with slurred speech. He stood slowly, steadying himself on the table. "Do you know the General gave you his wife's place next to him at dinner?" he asked. "He has left it open for her since she passed—until tonight."

As I returned to my room, I wondered what it meant. Another gesture of honor from the General? Maybe there was simply no other seat for me.

The laughter of several men was drifting through the open window, calling me to join them. I sat on the window, tucked safely in from the outside, where the Raven flew. In the courtyard below, torches flickered, casting patches of light. I craned my neck, checking the darker corners, finding them empty. I wanted to see the men who were laughing together. I yearned to share their merriment, as I had done at dinner.

In the starlit sky, a large black bird soared above, hanging high over the courtyard. Was it the Raven? Was it her? I squinted, but it flew too high in the sky to see clearly, so I closed the shutters and set the bar in place. I drifted to sleep, dreaming of the long black hair of the Walkyrie.

Power In Your Gentle Hand

I was not anxious to see Horse Master Gallo. I stood around the corner from the stables as the sun rose, hesitating to go there. I was sure he would insult me the moment he saw me, and I would not be able to control the anger of the Wulfhedinn. It would be better to walk into the stables and punch him in the nose immediately and be done with it. Maybe if I hit him *before* he angered me, I could keep the wolf at bay. It would come to that someday anyway, and we might as well get it over with, sooner rather than later. It was a good thing I had not gone to the armory first; I would have been aching to use my new blade.

A gentle hand touched my shoulder, and I unclenched my fists.

"May I join you?" asked Pyttel.

"Do you not have prayers to be making at this hour, monk?"

"There are always prayers to be made," he said. "God has given me leave to be with you this morning."

"Now you are my minder?"

"Have I not always been so?" He cackled. "Do not fret. I will not tell the General how a pious and humble man of God snuck up and surprised his Royal Huntsman."

I smirked. "You are a shifty monk. Your wit and skills must have served you well in your soldiering days."

"They serve me better now," he said.

I tried to say something curt but was grinning too hard.

He returned my smile. "I love appraising horseflesh, although my riding and killing days are over—"

"*Over?*" I asked, remembering his deft use of a blade when we had been attacked by bandits.

"In a manner of speaking. Anyway, Horse Master Gallo may have the disposition of a badger with a toothache, but he breeds and trains a fine mount." He gave me an impish wink. "Your encounter with him should be interesting."

"Perhaps you should go without *me*," I said.

"Oh no, no. That will not do. You are a part of the King's court now and must learn to interact with courtiers, even though Gallo is hardly a proper courtier. But none of the other nobles are as civilized as they pretend to be. Gallo has been kicked in the head too many times by his own horses, but at least he is honest about who he is. I am here to ensure all goes well with him."

He followed me to the stables. The smell of hay and manure grew thick as we hopped the fence. The training yard was filled with young shield bearers. They were skinny, beardless sons of noblemen. The Horse Master was tasked with preparing them to become elite Scola warriors. Instead, they scuttled around performing menial chores like servants. Several of them were repairing loose sticks in the wattle fence, and two were shoveling dung into an open handcart. One by one, they stopped working and stared at us.

The Horse Master spurred a huge black stallion out the stable door and charged past us, nearly knocking Pyttel over. His gruff voice boomed. "Get to work!"

The shield bearers scrambled back to their tasks.

"Are you as blind as you are stupid?" Gallo demanded of one small boy. "Why is my horse still stepping in shit?" He slid off his mount and took a couple of rickety steps on severely bowed legs. He grabbed the yoke, and threw the cart over in an intimidating show of strength. The boy and another youth sidestepped the cart but were splattered with manure.

"Now, maybe you will remember what shit looks like," Gallo said. He leaped on his horse and cantered across the yard toward several older youths who were weaving branches into the fence.

"This flimsy fence would not keep a pig contained," he said, kicking several holes in it. He grabbed a hefty branch off the top of the fence and wacked the boys. They tried to dodge his blows, but he cracked each one on the back.

"Stabilize those staves," he ordered, hitting them. "Tighten the wattle."

Pyttel shook his head. "He treats his horses better than his shield bearers. Most boys are trained to ride and fight by their own fathers, but many nobles want their sons to attend the famed Horse Master. They would be better off with their fathers."

"Depends on their fathers," I said.

"Yes, indeed," he said. "Learning discipline and enduring hardship is an important part of the training of a Scola warrior. I remember my youth as a shield bearer, the many nights I went to bed hungry and bruised. It toughened me and made me a better soldier, but these boys spend more time shoveling shit and toadying to Gallo's whims than they do training to fight. I am afraid their day will come too soon; the young ones will be called upon to attend Scola soldiers in battle, and the older ones will be made horsemen themselves. They will not be ready."

"When is a boy truly ready to kill another?" I asked.

He sighed. "You are right. No one is ever ready."

The Horse Master rode back across the yard toward us. "What do you want in my stables, woodsman?"

I was no expert in court etiquette, but calling me woodsman instead of my real title was a deliberate affront. I fought the urge to lash out at him. He towered over us on his horse, and I had no doubt he would try to run us down if provoked. I did not want Pyttel to get hurt.

"I came to choose a mount," I said.

Gallo harrumphed and pointed toward the closest stable. "Take your pick of the geldings in there, and do not bother me again."

Inside the stable, dust and the smell of wet straw hung thickly in the air. Several shield bearers were mucking the stalls, shoveling soiled straw into a cart. They stopped working and gaped at us.

"Royal Scout and Huntsman," the tallest one said with awe in his voice. He was a thin youth with a hungry look about him. He had broad shoulders and long bony legs and arms. He needed to be fed more to develop into a strong warrior.

The other shield bearers peeked at me through unkempt hair falling in their faces. The skinny youths all could have used an extra meal.

"The Royal Scout needs a good mount," said Pyttel.

"I am Ansgar, son of Count Erhard," the tall youth said with pride. "My father is cousin to the King and holder of many Rhineland estates to the north. I am to be made Scola soon. Horse Master Gallo has put me in charge of this stable. I will show you the best of the lot."

Gallo rode into the stable, and the boys scrambled back to work.

Gallo shook a gnarled finger at me. "I do not like the way my daughter looks at you. Stay away from her."

The Horse Master spurred away, forcing the smallest boy to jump out of his path. He landed in a pile of soiled straw, whimpering. He rolled over, revealing a large stain of dried blood back. He rose gingerly. Then his impish eyes sparked. "Have you *seen* his daughter? She has the mouth of a horse. Avoiding her will not be difficult." He pulled back his lips, imitating her large teeth, and made a retching sound.

The shield bearers laughed, and Pyttel covered a smirk by wiping his mouth on his sleeve. Gallo whipped his horse around, and the boys dodged into the stalls.

"Who said that?" Gallo demanded.

The boys hung their heads. The guilty boy bit his lip. Ansgar took a deep breath and hesitated, gathering his nerve. He was about to admit to the comment to protect the younger boy.

I stepped forward. "I said it."

Gallo glared at me. "You are a liar and a lowborn dirty dog," he said.

I loathed him and the way he spoke to me. I was unarmed, and Gallo carried a sword, but the wolf inside me did not care.

Howling in rage
Heart pounding, blood surging

Tear out his throat
Rip him to pieces

My arms and shoulders tensed, ready to grab his leg, yank him down, and pummel his face into pulp.

Pyttel stepped between us, raising his arms. "We are all soldiers of God," he said. "Let us try to remember our common calling."

Gallo sneered. "You are not at the King's table now, woodsman. This is my stable, and you will regret crossing me." He spat and reined his horse outside.

Heric and the other boys peeked from inside the stalls, beaming.

"Thank you, my lord, Royal Scout and Huntsman," said Ansgar, bowing his head. "The boy Heric has not learned to hold his tongue even though his back has not healed yet from his last beating." He scowled at Heric, who ducked back into the stall. "Now come, Royal Scout. Let me assist you in choosing a mount."

Ansgar walked along the line of stalls, pointing and commenting on each horse as we passed. "This one has gone lame. He is better now, but he is not ready to ride outside the training yard. The bay over there gets colic, and the gray in the next stall has no spirit—well, not enough spirit for you, Royal Scout," he said with a shy smile. "I would suggest the bay, a mare. She's young and willful, as spirited as a stallion, and she is strong and smart. Her step is agile, and she can maneuver well in brush and heavy forest. She is a good mount for the Royal Scout and Huntsman."

The mare threw her head and kicked the stall as we approached. The shield bearers followed us, watching us sheepishly.

"Finish mucking the stalls, boys," Ansgar ordered, "or there will be hell to pay when the Horse Master returns."

Everyone obeyed except Heric, who followed on my heel like a puppy.

Ansgar gently booted the boy on the arse. "Go get the Royal Scout a saddle and a bridle."

He ran to the saddle room, grinning smugly at the other boys.

Pyttel was eyeing the bay. "Horse Master Gallo told Tracker to pick a gelding, not a mare," he said.

"If you like," said Ansgar, "but I would take no less than this mare if I was the King's Royal Scout."

"You will have to endure the Horse Master's temper," I said.

Ansgar scoffed and puffed out his chest. "I am not afraid of him. I am to be made a Scola and become lord over my own estate next week."

Of course, it was easier for him to declare his mettle after his master had left, as youths were apt to do. It allowed him to practice courage before he became a Scola. Being a warrior was different from standing far behind the battle lines as a shield bearer. He would need every bit of bravery he could muster when he faced an enemy's charge for the first time.

On the far side of the stable, Heric struggled to carry a saddle that was nearly as big as he was. Ansgar went to help him.

The mare whinnied and kicked the stall. The whites of her eyes flashed. I murmured softly and let her smell my hand. Her breath was warm and smelled of oats. She calmed and allowed me to pat her neck and scratch her ears. She let me check her teeth, and I examined each of her hooves. They were free of cracks, and the iron shoes were set straight.

I looked at Pyttel over the mare's back. "I will never forget the Horse Master's threat," I said, releasing the leg.

"I did not think you would," he said, "but you can try."

"Why should I? He will not forget."

Pyttel leaned close and whispered so the boys could not hear him. "Because you have more power in your gentle hand than in the raging demon inside. Do you not see? You calmed this spooked mare with one touch."

I ran my fingers through her mane, and she turned to me and snorted softly.

"A gentle hand will not work with Gallo," I said. "He wields his position like a weapon against those who are weaker than he is. He will not browbeat me."

"Be wary of him—and always prepared to defend," said Pyttel, "but for your own sake, let some of your rage go." He lowered his voice so I could barely hear him. "Anger keeps the wolf close."

"Is that not what the King and the General want?" I shouted, startling the mare and the shield bearers.

Pyttel shushed me, feeding my frustration. Ansgar and Heric brought a bridle and saddle, wearing quizzical expressions, but I waved them off impatiently.

"But we saddle all the mounts of the King's courtiers," said Ansgar.

"I hate saddles and bridles with bits," I said, glaring at Pyttel.

I had not ridden since before I had been captured by the Saxons, but I leaped on the mare's back as if I did it every day. Ansgar opened the gate, and the mare jumped out of the stall with a light touch of my heels. She rode well, spirited and defiant, as anxious to escape the Horse Master as I was. Her temperament was well suited to mine; we carried each other well. I decided to call her Blitz because her spirit was like a bolt of lightning. Ansgar had indeed recommended a fine mount for me.

The Honor He
Never Had

After visiting the armory, I reported on horseback to General Theoderic. He silently appraised my armor and weapons. The armorer had equipped me as well as a Scola soldier. It was good to have a sword and dagger sheathed at my side again. I liked the well-balanced spear I carried, but the helmet and heavy mail armor felt confining. The weight of the armor was easy to bear, and it gave me the foreboding presence of an elite horseman, but I did not like it. The helmet shifted forward, rubbing against my nose. I had to juggle the spear into the hand holding the shield to push the helmet off my nose.

"You will get used to it," the General said as we passed through the gate onto the Hellweg.

I was not so sure.

"The mare suits you," he added.

We rode toward the King's garrison at Lippespringe. It was only a five-mile ride, but traffic on the road was heavy, and it took all morning to get there. The road was jammed with flocks of sheep, herds of cattle, and a line of oxcarts loaded with firewood. They were headed to Paderborn, and the General let them pass. Other nobles would have insisted the peasants yield to them, but he was too practical to wait. It was faster to let them pass, although there would be more fresh dung to step in. The stink of it was fierce as our horses' hooves mashed it into the dirt.

The General said little during the ride and did not mention my new duties. At the garrison, foot soldiers were digging ditches around the wall to strengthen its defenses. They stopped working and bowed to the General. After we passed, I felt their eyes lingering on my back.

Inside the garrison, the grounds were bustling with activity. Workers were building wattle and daub structures, and more soldiers were reinforcing the gate with iron stays. Lippespringe had the makings of a permanent garrison designed to train and support an entire army and withstand a siege. From this fortress, the King could rip a hole through the overgrown Teutoburg Forest and march his entire army into uncharted Saxon territory.

"Soon there will be nowhere for Widukind and his rebels to hide," said Theoderic.

I did not want to tell him there would always be a place for them to hide. I held my tongue and did not say it would take a hundred years to strip the entire Teutoburg Forest bare. There was no way to shed light in every dark corner of the pagan realm. Widukind and the Wulfhednar wielded forces he would never understand—and he knew it. He needed me and had made it my task to fight magic and demons. I longed to be far away from it all, but I would stay and do my duty, repaying the heathens threefold for what they had done to me.

We slept that night in the General's tent, which he used as his quarters and an office. The next morning, we took the Hellweg from Lippespringe northeast into the Teutoburg Forest.

"I want you to see it for yourself," he said.

The road soon narrowed, and the forest grew thicker around us. The shadows deepened, making us susceptible to ambush. The General was as well-appointed as I was, with a mail hauberk, helmet, sword, dagger, spear, and shield. A half dozen Scola horsemen accompanied us. Despite all this protection, I felt vulnerable and scanned the shadows repeatedly for signs of the rebels.

We passed a band of several dozen workers trudging down the road. They were guarded by six Scola riders and a company of infantry soldiers. About half of the workers were Frankish peasants. The others had the pale, round faces of Saxons. They carried shovels, pickaxes, and sawblades—tools the Saxons could use to overpower their guards if they chose. The Scola riders watched the Saxons and the edge of the forest, keeping their sword hands on their hilts. The infantry kept a tight grip on their shields and spears. They were all staying alert to signs of rebel attack and dissension among the Saxon road workers.

Had I seen some of these Saxons training at the Raven's Stones? Did any of them recognize me? It was difficult to tell. Any one of them might join the rebellion like so many of their kinsmen. They might have been working on the road so they could spy for Widukind. Maybe they were simply compliant, neither rebellious nor loyal to the King, just trying to survive.

A large man carrying a pickax was staring at me. He gripped his tool like a weapon and tipped it toward the soldiers. He raised his chin at me, as if inviting me to join him in attacking them. I was certain he knew who I was.

A growl rose in my throat.

The General was watching me. "What is it, Tracker? Do you sense something?"

I pointed to the Saxon with the pickaxe. "I do not like the big one."

General Theoderic reined his horse toward the soldiers. "Have him disarmed," he ordered.

"But General, he is the strongest of the lot," the captain said. "I need him to split and move rock."

"Let him shovel dirt with a spade."

One of the soldiers took the pickaxe from him. The Saxon glared at me, but it was not with hatred. I could contend with his loathing of me. He was invoking something more difficult to swallow, something the witch had said.

You are bound to me, to the pack
By blood, and by will
…if it be your will

I needed to get away from him, from all of them. I sank my heels into Blitz's ribs, and she leaped ahead. The General would not like that I had taken off without his leave, but he would not call after me like a mother hen in front of his men. I would contend with his reaction later in private. I did not care.

Within a couple of miles, the packed dirt of the road softened and grew damp. It soon turned into mud. I tried to steer around it, but the brush was so thick there was nowhere to go but through it. Blitz slowed to a walk, pulling her hooves from the muck until it became so deep she was forced to stop. From there, I could see the end of the road—a dead end engulfed by the forest.

Blitz snorted and pulled against the reins, wanting to turn back. I held her, but she fought me with all her strength. I stroked her withers, murmuring in her ear. She calmed a little, her eyes rolling at the trees. I turned her to draw her attention away from whatever was spooking her in the forest.

Wind in branches
Darkness behind sunny green leaf
Black wings flutter
…and are gone

With renewed power, Blitz lunged and bounded through the mud back to the dry road. She fought me, trying to gallop, but I held her to a canter and eventually slow her to a walk. She was breathing heavily, nostrils flaring, rib cage heaving. I murmured, stroking her until she quieted. I should have known she would sense the Raven. It would take time and training to get her accustomed to the Eater of Souls.

As I continued to calm her, the General trotted around a bend in the road and reined next to me. He was alone.

"You should not come here without your guard," I said. "This place is cursed."

"I am not afraid of them," he said, scanning the trees. "There was no swamp here until the rains came, and it hasn't drained since. It stretches a long way in every direction. Your job is to find a route around it." He tossed a large bag to me. Inside were dozens of strips of white linen. "Use these to mark the new route. I expect you to report back before the new moon."

I considered abandoning my mail hauberk and helmet until a sudden chilled breeze raised goose bumps on my neck. The extra protection would be worth a bit of extra discomfort. I tied the bag to my belt and handed Blitz's reins to the General.

"This horse is not ready for what lies in this forest," I said.

He raised his chin and his lips parted, as if he was going to speak. He might have thought briefly of the scouts he had lost in this forest. I paused to let him warn me to be careful, but he remained silent and turned back toward the garrison, leading Blitz.

Should Have Been Glad of It

I surveyed the dark trees and heavy brush at forest's edge.

No shadow of black wing
No scent of sweet musk and hawthorn

Heading into the trees, I chose a path that kept me twenty paces or more from the swampy area. I stayed on dry ground but tested each step before setting my full weight on it. It took far longer to do this than to walk straightaway, but I could not trust my eyes. All my senses were needed to keep my wits about me and not fall prey to the treacherous illusions in those woods.

I had to divert farther west than expected to avoid the swamp and find a route where the brush was thin enough to cut a road. I tied the white linen strips to branches every ten paces to mark the way. At a hundred paces, the forest had grown thicker, and it was more difficult to find a suitable route for a road. By the time I counted two hundred paces, I was detouring farther and father. At five hundred paces, I stopped counting.

The deeper I delved into the forest, the closer I was coming to the Walkyrie and her Wulfhednar, but I refused to let them frighten me. I had escaped them once, alone and unarmed. Now I was well armed and as protected as a Scola horseman. I was fearless—nearly.

I saw no sign of the Walkyrie or the Wulfhednar, but they knew I was there, marking a route into their forest. I stayed vigilant, ears perked for the distant sound of howling and the demonic shriek of the Raven. I sniffed for the taste of sweet musk and hawthorn, the scent of her body.

The Walkyrie
The Raven
Vala

I dropped the linen marker I was about to tie to a branch. With quivering fingers, I picked it up and dropped it again.

Why had I thought of her name? Why was I longing for her scent? The day before, she had been the witch, the black Raven, the Eater of Souls. Now I was thinking of her as the mystical warrior, the Walkyrie, and worse—Vala, the *woman*.

Sweat rolled down my forehead, and I wiped it away. Why did I care what I called her? No matter the name, I hated her.

Bound and naked
Powerless against the smell of her body

She rises and mounts
…sweet musk and flowers I cannot place…

I seek her smell
Yearn for it
Trace it into the past

The Walkyrie spurs
Her pelvis tight against mine
Saddling, seizing me without granting release
Pulled through boundless depths
Riding hard
Galloping across ground and sky

Sweet musk and hawthorn

Had I smelled it? My nostrils flared and sniffed, but her scent was gone. Perhaps it been carried away by the wind—or never there at all. I turned my nose, searching for a breeze that might carry a trace of her scent from the distance, from the Raven's Stones. The air was dead still, heavy with the odor of rotting leaves and wood. If she had been here, she was no longer.

I should have been glad of it, *should* have—

I moved through the forest, detouring farther to avoid the impenetrable thickets of hawthorn. Their flowers had bloomed out months ago, in early summer. I would not smell them now unless she was near. I both craved and dreaded their intoxicating fragrance. The pleasure of it was coupled with thorns that would pierce and trap me—as she had done.

After a long day, I had finally circumvented the entire swamp. Despite my efforts to find open spaces, the route was barely passable. I was forced to squeeze between thickets and trees in many places. It would take a long time to clear a road wide enough for an army to pass, and I feared the forest would engulf my little path long before that. The General would not be pleased.

I retraced my steps. Would my markers be there, or had the Raven or her bewitched forest hidden them already? I was relieved to find the markers were intact. I made crosses from branches fastened with strips of cloth and planted several along the way, hoping they would keep the dark spirits at bay.

Night had fallen by the time I returned to the garrison. The Saxon workers and several detachments of Frankish foot soldiers had finished working for the day and were making camp. Every eye was on me as I walked to the General's tent.

He listened intently while I described the length of the detour and the thick brush that needed clearing. When I finished, he grunted once.

"Any sign of the rebels?" he asked.

"No sign of them at all."

Honor Among His Own

Someone whistled. It almost sounded like a bird, but it had a human tone to it. A signal for attack? It was near dawn—the perfect time for the rebels to launch an assault on the garrison.

I jumped from sleep to my feet, grabbing my sword belt. The General's pallet was empty. Where had he gone? I rushed out of the tent, listening intently. The whistling drew nearer, sounding more like a lively tune than a disguised birdcall. The whistler was enjoying the tune, as if returning from a night at the brothel.

"Arise, Tracker! No daylight to lose." It was the General.

I had not imagined he could whistle, but I doubted he had visited the brothel. The smell of roasting pork drifted toward me, and my mouth watered. All was well in the garrison.

"Several dozen free Frankish farmers arrived from the Rhineland last night," the General said. "Saxons who owe service to the King reported too. There are more than I expected—a good sign. Every Saxon working here is one less warrior fighting for the rebels. Some hefty fellows they are too. I should have enough muscle now to recoup lost time and skirt the swamp quickly." One corner of one his tight upper lip raised in a near smile. "But first we eat. It is going to be a long day."

I buckled the sword belt around my waist, doubting any number of stout men could clear the entire route as fast as he hoped. I did not tell him that the Raven might have carried away his markers or that the forest might have overgrown my narrow route. When he turned away, I rested my hand on my cross, summoning faith in the other crosses I had planted along the way.

We broke our fast with bread, cheese, and beer. He ordered larger portions than I had expected. As I ate my fill, servants dropped a platter of roasted pork in front of us. I was no longer hungry, but my mouth watered. I grabbed a shank and hesitated, remembering Pyttel's crooked face and the foolish rules he had taught me about courtly behavior. I dropped it, waiting for the General to begin first, but he waved me on.

"Eat all you can," he said. "I want you well-fed and strong. I am sending you into the forest to patrol today." He nibbled on a few spare bites, while I devoured pork until I had to loosen my belt.

Soon after, we met with Horse Master Gallo, who had arrived with his shield bearers from Paderborn. He was training them in a small corral. The General instructed Gallo to have the shield bearers ready and close at hand to attend the Scolas in case of a rebel uprising on the road.

In the corral, a youth of about thirteen years clung to the back of a large unbroken stallion. It rubbed the boy's leg against the fence and bucked. The youth flew off and landed in the dirt with a groan.

The Horse Master spat through his missing teeth and hobbled on his bowed legs toward the fallen youth. Instead of checking on him, he grabbed the stallion's reins and leaped onto its back like a man half his age with straight legs. As difficult as it was for him to walk, he rode with remarkable ease. His gnarled hands and strong legs guided the horse through a series of controlled paces around the stable yard. The spirited mount obediently walked, trotted, and cantered to his commands. Gallo was the Horse Master, the man who could breed and train a horse better than anyone in the King's kingdom—and he made sure I saw it.

I hated him as he rode around the yard, ignoring the boy who had fallen. The boy rose, no worse for wear, but the Horse Master's actions gnawed at me. I had not seen him raise a hand to his proud horses, but his shield bearers scampered about him like beaten dogs.

I spotted Heric, the smallest shield bearer. He was pulling a handcart full of tools across the yard. Bent over, he shuffled and struggled to move the cart like a crippled old man. He looked at me but did not flash his impish smile. His face was pale, and he was trembling. He turned, and I saw fresh blood soaking through the back of his shirt. The Horse Master had taken the whip to him again.

Blood running down my back
Pouring from shredded flesh
Hanging like red ribbons

The scars on my back tightened and ached with the memory. The pain was horrible, but it was easier to forget than the humiliation and the anger. The Wulfhedinn had ripped apart my tormentor and watched as he choked on his own blood.

Now, I wanted to lash the Horse Master with his own whip until he begged for mercy and fell dead.

Its beating heart steals inside me
Peering through the eyes of the beast
Pounding harder and harder
Muscles surge
Strength rules
A growl rises
Wulfhedinn

"Do not concern yourself with that boy," the General said harshly. "Save your demon fury for the rebels."

He startled me, driving away the wolf and summoning back the Royal Scout. Until now, Pyttel had been the only one who could deter the wolf.

The General was watching me closely. "The boy's defiance must be broken if he is to become a Scola rider one day," he said. "He must have respect for his commanders and follow orders. Let us hope this time he has learned."

"He has only learned to hate his commanders," I said.

"He needs to focus his fury at the enemy, as do you. If he does not come to understand honor among his own, he will be sent back to his noble family in disgrace. It will be a black mark against him—for life."

I did not know the kind of honor he spoke of, but I did understand shame. I could not bear to think of about it any longer, so I straightened my back and rode proudly with the General—and made sure Gallo saw it.

Talk of Demons

The Lippespringe guards opened the gate and watched us leave. Outside several dozen free peasants from the Rhineland stood along the road, leaning on their tools. They were attended by a band of Scola riders who were nervously eyeing the fringes of the forest.

Pyttel was there, offering a prayer to a kneeling peasant. He made the sign of the cross and smiled at me with a wicked curl of his lips.

The General called the captain aside. "Why are they not working?" he asked.

"They are waiting their turn for a blessing from the monk," the captain said.

"It will take half the morning. Tell the monk to give one blessing for all and get on with the work."

"I tried, but they refuse to begin without special devotions of protection."

"Make them," the General snapped.

"They say they have seen demons—wolf demons—in the shadows in the forest. They are certain this place is cursed."

"Nonsense."

"But, my lord, some of the Scola riders have seen them too." His mouth hung open, as if he was unsure he should say more. He scratched his chin and lowered his voice. "I caught a glimpse of them myself this morning—eyes glowing, staring out from the trees."

The General glanced around in a perfunctory manner. "You are letting shadows and the hysterics of ignorant peasants trick your mind. You saw wolves, not demons."

"Wolves do not stand upright and carry axes, my lord," he said softly, without defiance.

"You half-witted pignut! You saw either rebels or bandits, who are no match the finest force of horsemen in Europe."

"Yes, General."

General Theoderic glowered at him. "The Royal Scout has patrolled far into the forest and found no sign of danger. He marked a safe route for the road and will continue to patrol. Now, put a stop to these ridiculous rumors, and get the peasants working."

"Yes, my lord." He waved his arms at Pyttel and shouted, "Enough, monk! Enough! Make one quick blessing for all."

Both the peasants and the soldiers became restless, murmuring to one another.

"The woods have been scouted and the way is clear," the captain said. "There will be no more talk of demons. Anyone spreading such lies will be flogged."

The crowd grew more restless. Pyttel moved to the front of the crowd and raised his hands. "My children, be comforted!"

he said. "Submit yourselves therefore to God. Resist the Devil, and he will flee from you."

A calm air slowly fell over them as Pyttel made a quick blessing. Then the solders resumed their watch, and the peasants hoisted their tools, hacking as brush, dirt and rock. I marveled at how quickly Pyttel could restore faith in men who were shaken by fear.

It was not lost on the General. "Sometimes I think the lunatic monk can control my soldiers better than my captains can."

"He was a soldier himself," I said, "and now he has the ear of God."

"Or the Devil," he said.

Was he aware of Pyttel's secret visits to the pagan spring and his sacrilegious sacrifices to Wodan? If he was, he would not reveal the truth as long as it served him—like the truth about me. I scratched my moustache, troubled at the thought.

The General turned to me. "Scout the immediate area today and report back. There are more crews working farther ahead. Check on their progress, and tell me what they are talking about."

I left Blitz to one of the guards. It would be easier to patrol and remain undetected by the Wulfhednar on foot. I did not like wearing the helmet and mail armor. It was hot and would not blend into the forest well, like a simple brown mantle—or my wolf skin—but I kept the mail on.

I scanned the trees and the shadows along the road. I had no doubt the soldiers and workers had seen them, but I sensed the wolf warriors had since left the area, biding their time.

I passed more crews of workers and soldiers. Many of the laborers had stripped to the waist. Their backs glistened with sweat as they cut and hauled undergrowth from the forest into huge piles. Some were setting fire to the slash. They had made much progress during the morning, and no one talked about anything unusual.

I was unsure what I would find where the road stopped and the swamp began. I expected my cloth markers would be gone. The Walkyrie would not leave them to mark the King's road into her territory. When I arrived, I was surprised to find the first one tied to the branch, fluttering in the breeze. Another road crew had been there and had cut a wider path through the forest past the marker. They were making rapid progress to the second marker, and the ground had stayed dry under them, proving my route to be a solid one. The path was not broad enough yet to allow an army to march through, but widening it further would not take long now.

There was a smug grin on the face of the captain in charge of this group, as if every tree and bush they cut down was a rebel they slew. At this rate, they would circumvent the swamp in several days. They would be headed directly toward the Raven's Stones, the heart of the Saxon rebellion. All was well.

I was glad to have good news to report to the General later. I was proving him correct. No one had seen wolf demons, just wolves or bandits. I did not believe it though, so I stayed vigilant as I headed into the forest to patrol.

A Blessing from Wodan

A gray cloud had hung over the western sky all morning. By midday, it had grown subtly and was moving closer. By late afternoon it covered the entire sky. The air cooled slightly, almost imperceptibly. A tiny breeze turned a leaf or two and faded. The forest remained quiet until the evening horn blew. It blared through the trees, calling everyone inside. Under the thick cloud cover, darkness was falling fast, and no one wanted to be locked out for the night.

I followed the last of the workers and soldiers to the garrison. I had promising news and was anticipating a good meeting with the General. Progress on the road around the swamp was better than expected, and I had not detected a trace of the Wulfhednar all day. I had circled around to the place where they had been sighted near the front gate and did not find a single broken twig or crushed blade of grass where they had reportedly stood. I did not smell their rotting fur skins or the scent of the Walkyrie, sweet musk and hawthorn.

Before passing through the gate, I surveyed the edges of the forest. Nothing stirred but a few leaves hit by drops of falling rain. The timber gate creaked shut behind me, and the guards lowered the bar with a loud thud. As soon as we were locked in, lightning flashed. It struck the garrison wall with a deafening crack, as if it had broken open the earth. The strike knocked several soldiers off the wall and ignited the timbers. A huge orange blaze erupted.

"Fire on the wall! Fire on the wall!" soldiers called as they rushed to the fallen.

Their voices were drowned out by booming thunder that rattled the gate on its hinges. Men ran to the well with buckets, and I joined them. Before we could fill more than a couple of buckets, the sky unleashed a deluge and put out the fire.

I returned to the General's tent. He was standing in the door, staring at the smoldering wall. He grunted once when I gave my report, but he was not listening.

The lightning and thunder exhausted themselves, but the rain kept pouring. The temperature dropped as if winter had come early.

Water was pooling on the tent roof, seeping through the fabric and threatening to collapse it. I ran outside and pulled out two tent poles to lower the edge of the roof. The water flowed off it with a cold splash at my feet. I staked the poles and moved our pallets to the driest spot inside the tent.

It rained all night, and when I woke, my pallet was nearly soaked by the ice-cold water running under the tent. The General was at the door, watching men slip in the mud between the rows of tents. Despite the deluge, he ordered the road crews back to work. They left the garrison shivering. The relentless rain flowed off their woolen mantles but would soon soak through to their skin, chilling their bones. I did not need to hear their grumbling. I knew what they were saying, and I had little hope my route through the forest was still open and not swallowed up by the forest.

"Tracker, I want you to patrol today, but stay close to the road," the General said.

He gave me a cloak made of wool that had been pounded and treated to become felt. It was an expensive mantle worn by the rich, and it would resist the rain longer than regular wool. I thanked him and threw it over my armor.

The road had turned into a quagmire. The soggy workers complained and glared at me as I passed them. They envied my felt cloak and thick-soled boots. At the end of the road, I was glad to see my path had not been overtaken by forest or swamp. It was muddy but passable. The white markers were also intact, wet and dripping.

I saw no sign of the rebels. They were probably waiting out the weather, staying warm and dry, waiting for fever and sickness to attack the King's army for them. Unless the rain stopped soon, it would not take long for fits of coughing to spread through the garrison. More soldiers died this way than by fighting, and everyone dreaded succumbing slowly to the death rattle.

The rain continued throughout the day and into the night. The next morning, the General ordered the workers to go back out, as he did for the next several days. The rains did not cease, the mud got worse, and progress on the road slowed to a crawl.

I had never seen so much mud. There was mud that was mostly water, and water that was mostly mud. It ran down the road and through the garrison in rivulets. Deep puddles of stagnant mud made low-lying areas impossible to cross. Men and horses slipped on slimy mud, and clay-like mud clung to feet and horses' hooves like mortar. There was mud mixed with rock and gravel and mud mixed with dung and human shit. There was black mud, brown mud, and gray mud.

Everything was soaked—clothing, boots, food, pallets, and tents. Even my felt cloak could not keep out the rain forever. Water finally soaked through, and it stunk like a rotten sheep carcass. The icy wetness saturated my clothes, penetrating my skin and bones.

One day, I was traversing the forest near one of the peasant work crews. They were standing in the mud, taking their mid-day rest. I crept closer to hear them talk. Some of them were coughing and complaining of fever. Backs bent with weariness, they chewed their sodden crusts of bread.

A tall man with a round face spat. "These rains will be the end of me," he said with a heavy Saxon accent. "I have no dry place to sleep, and now my bread has gone moldy. My fields of rye are rotting because not there to harvest them."

"All our crops must be flattened into the mud by now," said a thin man whose teeth were chattering.

"My bread ran out yesterday," said another, "and I still owe another week's service."

"I will starve here breaking my back to build this road," said the thin man.

"The road to nowhere," said the tall one, staring at his bread in the mud. "It is the cursed Frankish King and his God who brings this misfortune upon us."

"No, do you not see?" asked a wizened, gray-haired Saxon. "The rain is a blessing from Wodan. It is slowing our work on the King's road into our lands. The General will be forced to stop it now."

"And yet my family will starve this winter," said the tall Saxon.

"No, Widukind and the Wulfhednar will not let that happen," the old one said. "Wodan is with them. They will drive these Christian dogs from our lands and take back everything stolen from us. No Saxon will starve."

"Yes, Widukind will feed those who are loyal to him—but where do we stand?" asked the third man. "We are acting like the King's slaves, obeying his decrees and whims."

"My harvest is ruined. I will have more to gain by joining the rebellion than by staying loyal and starving this winter," said the tall one.

"What about our families?" another worker piped in. "If we join the rebellion, they will have to go into hiding in the forest, and they will not survive the winter. I have young ones, and my wife is with child."

"We must wait for the nobles to join with Widukind," said the old man. "Then we could not lose."

"Our nobles do not care about us," said the tall man. "They are loyal to the Frankish king, who gives them titles and lands and lines their purses with silver."

The old man pulled his sodden mantle tighter about his shoulders. "Widukind is a noble," he said.

"He *was* a noble. Now he is an outlaw, without lands, without title."

The old man rubbed his bent back. "We must take solace in knowing the Franks are not getting their fields harvested either, and the King's army cannot fight on an empty stomach."

The Demon Remains Close

The weather did not deter the General—until it hailed. It pelted us with balls of ice the size of walnuts, as if someone was throwing rocks at my face. No matter which direction I turned, I could not avoid them. The General finally ordered the work to stop, and everyone returned to the Lippespringe garrison to take shelter until the weather passed. It was the worst hailstorm anyone had ever seen.

When it passed, the General ordered everyone back to the road. I escorted the first crew to continue work on the path I had marked. All was quiet on our journey there, but when we arrived at the spot, a sudden wind blew in more black clouds. The hair stood on the back of my neck, and I jumped as lightning struck a rotting oak tree next to me. The sound of the crack was deafening, and the tree crashed before anyone realized what was happening. The huge trunk crushed three foot soldiers, burying them completely in the mud. Everyone rushed to move it, although the foot soldiers could not possibly have survived.

It began to rain, and the nearby Lippe River overflowed its banks. Water washed over the road and my path as if a damn had broken. We sank to our thighs in the fast-running muddy current and scrambled to climb to higher ground as the water rose.

Reluctantly, the General gave the order stop work.

"It will take days to chop it into pieces that can be hauled away, even in dry weather," he muttered, rain dripping down his mantle.

The Lippespringe garrison had flooded, leaving tents floating in a lake of muddy water. The General was unhappy about it, but we had no choice but return to Paderborn. I did not like it either. How long would we have to wait there for the rain to stop and the floodwater to recede? I dreaded being trapped with him in his quarters in the palace. After a day back at the palace, I was hoping he would dismiss me to my room, but he did not. And it kept raining.

"Is this all the witch's doing?" he asked, staring out his dripping window.

"I do not know," I said.

"Go and find out," he said. "Put a stop to it."

I almost relished the idea of going out in the weather. It gave me a purpose, and anything was better than staying there and enduring the General's endless silent brooding.

I set out with my cloak. It was saturated now, but it kept me warm. The guards laughed and shook their heads as they opened the gate for me. They thought I was mad for leaving the shelter of Paderborn. They might have envied me for my position in the past, but their smug sniggering told me they were content to be humble men-at-arms that day. No one wanted to be a scout anymore, not after so many had been lost, and not in this weather.

I headed straight into the forest, where the mud was not as bad as it was on the road. My first task was to find a way to get around the flooded section of the road.

After several miles, the rain eased to a drizzle, and the sun peeked out. I dropped the hood. For a moment, sunshine warmed my face while tiny droplets wettened it. I glimpsed part of a rainbow above the trees, and soon the rain stopped.

Despite the warming day, I shivered as I neared the place where the dead soldiers lay rotting under the fallen tree. I doubted the water had risen high enough to loosen and shift the huge tree, but if it had, their remains might wash up later downstream, or never be found at all.

The wind shifted slightly, and I smelled the putrid scent of decaying flesh. I sniffed. It was not a human smell, but I did not have to see it to recognize it.

Rotting horseflesh

I climbed a small rise where I could see the fallen tree. Above it, hung a nithing horse, a Saxon curse pole, one of the strongest forms of pagan magic. The rebels had spiked the head on a thick branch of the fallen tree. The horsehide was draped behind it, legs and hooves dangling in the breeze. It hung in the air like a ghost.

Galloping
Trampling the bodies of crushed soldiers beneath the water
Its empty eyes staring at me
Cursing me

I had never wanted to see another dreadful nithing horse. Earlier that summer, the rebels had staked one near Paderborn to curse the King. We had destroyed it, but it had still brought the King bad fortune in building his road. This one was different. It was staked on the King's road, but its dark magic was directed at me. Widukind, the witch, and their pack of Wulfhednar were threatening me.

The wolf howls inside
Heart pounding, blood surging
Rip it to pieces
Rip them all to pieces

In a fury, I bounded into the icy water, sinking to my hips. The cold shocked me, clearing my head and chasing the wolf away. I stopped, deciding to leave the curse pole stand. The General would want to see this for himself.

He slammed his fist into the table when I told him about it that evening. "Show me," he said.

"We should bring an escort of horsemen," I said.

"No. I want no one else to know of this."

I understood. He did not want any more rumors of pagan demons and magic spreading through the workers and soldiers. And there were other concerns.

"But Widukind and the Wulfhednar are close," I said. "It is too dangerous for the King's General to go—"

"No," he snapped. "You are a Wulfhedinn. You are all I need."

"Pyttel," I said. "We need Pyttel."

"The monk?"

"Bring the man who has God's ear," I said. "He is good with a blade as well."

He agreed, and we rode out of Paderborn the next day—a General, a monk, and a Wulfhedinn. Some of the water had drained since the rains had stopped, but the road was still muddy. When we arrived at the fallen tree, the General remained quiet. His mind was busy weighing his anger and calculating his next move.

Pyttel crossed himself several times. "Blessed Mother of God," he said. "I feared something like this."

"Get rid of it," the General said, as if he wanted me to drown an unwanted cat.

I spurred Blitz into the water, but she reared, refusing to go closer. I left her with Pyttel and waded through the muddy water myself. Climbing onto the massive trunk, I inched close to the branch where the nithing horse hung.

Flies swarmed around the wet, rotting flesh. I moved closer, holding branches to keep my balance on the trunk. I flipped the heavy hide over the branch, catching it on another branch. I had to yank it with all my strength to break it loose. More stink wafted from the carcass as it fell, but I ignored it and kicked off the horse head. It landed in the water, splashing me.

"Pyttel, you will accompany Tracker," said the General. "Do whatever you must to ensure it is never found. Tomorrow, we will haul away the tree and retrieve our dead. Then work will continue without further delay."

He returned to Paderborn, insisting he did not need a guard, and he was probably right. The Wulfhednar were not after him—not yet. They were threatening me.

I dragged the wet carcass out of the water and rolled the skin around the head. Tying a rope around the bundle, I dragged it behind me. Blitz was restless but controllable. Hiding the head had settled her, as it had me.

Pyttel followed, keeping his distance behind the nithing horse. I searched for a nearby place that was hidden from the road—a place where a Christian would not likely tread.

The ground rose to the north of the road. I spurred Blitz up the rise and surveyed the other side of the hill. The forest below was thick and ominous, fenced by impenetrable thickets of hawthorn. The moisture from the rains was rising, creating a light mist that blanketed the area.

I stopped and sniffed but did not catch the scent of sweet musk and hawthorn. She was not there.

Pyttel had reined his mount next to me. Peering curiously at me he said, "Your eyes are dark and angry. Is the wolf rising in you?"

"They have set their curse against me."

He crossed his arms. "Stop your vexing. They were trying to scare the peasants with the nithing horse. Nothing more. Not everyone is trying to curse you. Did it ever occur to you that when you allow the wolf to possess your heart, you are *summoning* the Eater of Souls to you?"

I had heard him but refused to listen. He sounded like a nagging fishwife.

"She cannot take me," I said. "She does not command me."

"Who does command you?"

"No one."

"Not the King? The General? Not even God?"

"No one," I repeated. I handed him Blitz's reins and the rope dragging the bundled nithing horse. "Bury it in those thickets."

He snorted. "Down *there*? By *myself*? You must come with me."

"I must do something else," I said. "You will be safe. They are not here."

"Burying the nithing horse will not break the curse."

"Say a prayer, sacrifice to the old gods—rub your cock on it. It has worked for you in the past."

He scoffed and grabbed my arm. "You do not intend to go after them?" His grip tightened on my arm like a rope twisted by a stout stick. "You cannot go into the forest alone. They are drawing you into the wood. Do you not see it? They want you to call upon the Wulfhedinn, to use your anger rashly, to follow them blindly."

"She—they will not take me a second time."

"Heed my words," he said. "You have been redeemed, but the demon remains close to you. Even now, your face blazes with the wolf's dark rage. You cannot defeat the Eater of Souls so easily. You have too much to lose now—your place of high honor in the King's court and in God's Kingdom."

"And I could lose your place in heaven, as well, Brother?"

He shoved my arm away. "Blessed God, Gerwulf!"

"Do not call me by that name. I am Tracker, King Karl's Royal Scout and Huntsman."

"You have battled through untold tortures and come out victorious. Do not throw it all away now with recklessness."

"You are afraid they will take me, and I will not return."

"Yes, I am afraid," he said. "I fear you may *choose* not to return."

Fallen Fool

I ran into the trees without glancing back.

"Beware!" Pyttel called after me. "Take great care! Do not to listen to her!"

I headed northeast and caught the Wulfhednar's scent quickly. It led me deeply into the woods to where I had marked the new route for the road. As I had feared, it was hidden by creeping vines and prickly brush.

"Cursed witch," I murmured.

I pushed through the brush, looking for the next marker— gone.

Their scent hanging, lingering
Wolf hides
Hot breath of beasts hungry for blood

Sweet musk and hawthorn

Ten paces beyond, the next marker was also missing, and the next and the next. I did not have to take another step; she had taken them all.

I drew my sword. The wind blew, lightly at first, growing into large gusts. It whipped my hair and bent sapling trees. Above the din, I heard her call.

Shrieking
Like ice on my neck
Like death on my shoulder

Black wing soaring
Black as midnight
White linen marker hanging from her beak
Carried away into the gale

Branches waved wildly, the gusts tearing leaves from their limbs. Dirt and grit blew into my eyes, blinding me. The cross thrashed against my chest, threatening to tear lose. Hail pelted my cheeks with shards of ice.

I squared my shoulders against the windstorm and stood strong against her, denying her. She could beat me with her savage winds and stinging hail. It was the kind of pain that distracted me from the anguish inside, if only for a moment. I wanted the icy balls to pelt me, to cut me. I wanted to feel it and not back down. I would prevail against her maelstrom. I had fought and survived it before. Now I would triumph.

"I am here!" I shouted into the wind. "Show yourself! Witch, Walkyrie, Raven, Eater of Souls, face me now as all of them!"

She hangs
Floating above on the air
As if there is no wind at all

"I dare you to challenge me if you are so powerful! Take me if you can."

The scent of the Wulfhednar was all about, coming from every direction in the swirling squall.

…and sweet musk and hawthorn

"Show yourself! Fight me!"

I yelled until my throat grew hoarse, but no one appeared to accept my challenge. I continued shouting until my voice became a guttural call.

Howling
Against her
…and the storm she brings

The wolf's beating heart steals inside me
Pounding harder and harder
Muscles surge
Strength rules

Her black wings flap
Once, twice, three times…

I bounded after her through the trees like a beast on the hunt. I followed her southwest, toward the heathen spring near the Lippespringe garrison. The pagans called it Wodan's Spring and had sacrificed to the god in its sacred waters—until King Karl seized it to wash the filth of his courtiers.

Soft light filters through the budding tree branches
Radiant blue funnel, flowing with sacred waters
Reflects everything
Sees everything
Eye of Wodan

Pyttel was now the only one who sacrificed there. His sacrilegious act was alive and undeniable in my mind. The mad monk had taken a bite of the goat's heart, thanking Wodan for his blessings. Pouring the goat's blood over his head, he had rubbed it all over his naked body—his erect penis red with it.

Despite this—or because of it—I followed the Walkyrie's scent there. It grew stronger and more powerful with each step, intoxicating me with the fury of the wolf.

Perched on a tree
Linen strips hanging on bare dead branches
…my markers
Blowing in the breeze

Under the tree
She floats
In a thin linen gown
Draping over her breasts and buttocks
Ray of sun shining through
Black hair loose over her shoulders
Crowned by a ring of dripping white flowers
Sweet musk and hawthorn…
Vala

Reaching for her
The touch of her skin
The scent of her hair
…aching with rage and desire

The tree blooms
Tiny white flowers
White ribbons
Fluttering in the soft breeze
In the tree
In her hair
Vala

…turning red
Dripping with blood

The wind calmed. She was gone, and the markers had vanished. My mind slowly cleared, leaving an aching in my loins.

The Eye of Wodan stared at me from the center of the spring, casting a glow that hung over the rippling water like a ghost. I dodged behind a thicket, but the Eye had seen me, my weakness, my failure. I had been tempted by her, tricked by her—again. Even without my wolf skin, I had summoned the beast and let it take ahold of me.

I should have heeded the monk's warning, but I had fallen fool to the Eater of Souls. Her plan was obvious now; she led me away from those I had sworn to protect. Now their blood would flow. Iron-clad soldiers and the workers they guarded had no chance against an ambush by the witch and her Wulfhednar.

I bounded back through the forest toward the fallen tree. The work crew would be there to clear it by now, and the General might be with them.

The wolf's beating heart
Pounding harder and harder
Muscles surge
Strength rules

I could think of only one thing…
Pyttel.

Jf Jt Be Your Will

I ran as fast as my feet could carry me. The Wulfhednar would attack them at dusk, and the fool monk would try to fight them.

It was too far to get there to warn the General, but I might make it in time to help defend the attack. I thrust my body forward, feet bounding over the ground with every bit of energy I could muster.

Faster and faster
Two legs…four
Faster and faster

Sweat poured from my forehead, running down my neck, but I pushed harder. As I neared the road, I heard iron tools chopping and hacking at trees and brush. Workers were talking as they labored. The Wulfhednar had not attacked yet! I drew my sword. I was close, a hundred paces away…seventy-five paces…fifty…

A shriek echoes through the forest
Like ice on my neck
Like death on my shoulder
The wind rises
Carrying the scent of sweet musk and hawthorn

A whoosh of arrows sailed over my head toward the road. A moment later, horses whinnied and screams rang through the forest as the arrows pierced armor and sank into flesh.

The Walkyrie rides
Raven's head and woman's breasts
Wings stretched
She lands and charges
Hooves pounding
Knocking me aside

The pack follows
Their howls pierce the forest
Bounding on four legs
Leaping over me

The screams from the road grew louder, shrill and panicked. Weapons clanged. Deeper shouts rang out, soldiers calling defensive orders. I smelled people hidden behind me in the trees, probably the rebel archers, but there was no time to worry about them. I scrambled to my feet and ran to the road.

Taken by surprise, most of the Scola soldiers had fallen before they could raise their shields. Arrows were lodged in their chests, faces, and throats. Some moved, feebly attempting to limp or crawl away. A few clung to their swords, but they quickly hit by another volley of precisely aimed arrows.

The Wulfhednar leaped at the Scola soldiers who remained on their horses.

Demon eyes
Fangs dripping
Snapping
Snarling

They sunk their spears into the backs and flanks of the riders and pulled them off their mounts. Steel cleaved through flesh and bone. Their axe blades hacked deeply into the fallen, again and again, until God Himself would not recognize them.

The Frankish workers were fleeing toward the garrison. The Saxon workers, emboldened by the Wulfhednar's attack, rose in rebellion and attacked the foot soldiers with picks and shovels. Outnumbered five to one, many of the infantrymen froze in shock and panic.

The General reined his horse, shouting at his infantry. "Fight!"he ordered, blocking a Wulfhedinn's axe blow with his sword. "Fight!"

The Saxon workers encircled the foot soldiers, beating and pounding them with their iron tools. The large Saxon I had stripped of the pickaxe smashed several heads with his spade. He retrieved a fallen spear and jammed it through the ribcage of another foot soldier. Yanking out the spear, he stabbed another soldier through the throat with it.

The Scola captain clung weakly to his horse, arrows lodged in his hip and shoulder. Blood seeped through the rings in his mail coat, and he had dropped his sword. A Wulfhedinn bounded at him swinging a long axe. Swoosh! One chop and the captain's head fell, the body collapsing after it.

The General was the last rider still on his horse. He reined around. Sword poised, he charged the nearest Wulfhedinn. Another volley of arrows pelted the soldiers. The General ducked behind his shield, but his horse was hit in the shoulder. It reared, whinnying and lurching. His strong hands kept tight control on the reins, and he stayed in the saddle with the balance of a man half his age.

The Walkyrie and several Wulfhednar circled around him, staying clear of the horse's kicking hooves. He calmed the animal enough to poise his sword, threatening to slash anyone who came near. He was a fearsome sight, every bit the King's finest General, until an arrow hit him in the thigh. The impact nearly knocked him off the horse, but he held on, clutching at his saddle as the Wulfhednar closed in on him.

Without thought, I howled, drawing attention to myself. The Wulfhednar turned, and the Walkyrie spurred her black stallion toward me. The General retreated to the garrison, clinging to his horse's neck. He did not look back.

The Walkyrie charged, a mantle of sleek black feathers flying behind her. Swirls of black paint covered her body. Her long black hair was knotted and pulled high away from her spear arm. She aimed her spear at my chest, cold dead eyes piercing through the Raven's mask. She was the Eater of Souls, and I was just another Frank to kill.

I widened my stance and raised my sword, but she stopped her mount short of my blade. It snorted and pawed the ground. Her strong arms held the horse to circling around me.

"So, you have fled back to their God." She drew close enough to thread her spear through the leather strip holding my cross. It scraped my skin as she threatened to thrust the blade through my chest.

"Witch." I glowered.

"I am the *Walkyrie*." Her voice was as hard and cold as the steel of her spear tip. "And you are still Wulfhedinn, Gerwulf."

"Liar, deceiver," I spat.

She leveled her spear tip at my throat, the point pressing into my skin. The Wulfhednar circled around us.

Fangs dripping
Snapping
Snarling

They moved closer, tightening the circle. I tried to focus on them all, but she pulled my gaze deeply into her lifeless eyes. For a moment, she locked me there, as if I was bound helplessly in her stone tower again. Then she withdrew her spear from my throat, releasing me. I spun around, my sword poised, trying to guard against them all while searching for the one I wanted to kill.

The largest Wulfhedinn stepped forward. The wolf mask covered most of his face, but I recognized his scent. I had tracked it for King Karl, a mix of sweat—from wielding heavy weapons—and of blood and death.

Widukind
Leader of the Saxon rebellion
Leader of the Wulfhedinn pack

Now I would fulfill my duty to the King and to God. I would kill him, and his wolf warriors would kill me. I did not care. My soul would finally escape the Raven and join God in Heaven while she carried the beast in me to Hell.

I sprang at Widukind, aiming the tip of my sword at his chest. He leaped away, dodging my thrust. I swung, but he evaded my blade a second time—and did not counterattack. The other Wulfhednar stood ready, but they kept their distance and did not jump into the fight.

Widukind's eyes bore through the wolf mask, dark with rage, like mine. I howled and thrust at his neck, but he fended off my blow with the flat of his sword. The impact had no effect on him. No man could have stood against a direct hit from my bone-crushing blade, but he was no ordinary man. He was a Wulfhedinn, the demon who had created me.

"Fight!" I jumped and swung, putting the weight of my whole body into it. He blocked the strike, but the impact knocked the mask off his face.

I had seen this face before, in the looking glass and in the reflection in quiet streams and pools of water. I had seen it in myself. The moments vanished, the scar on my chest burning with the memory.

From the longest day
Far into the Raven's night...

Drums beating, beating, beating
Let his blood mix with that of all the pack

"Fight me!" I cried, aiming to stab him through his bare chest.

He opened his arms wide, exposing the Wulfhedinn scar that matched my own. "Do what you must. You are not a lamb of the Christian God. You have the heart of a wolf warrior of Wodan."

He had revealed himself, made himself vulnerable, yet his power over me was undeniable.

Father
Bound to me
If it be your will

I hesitated, my sword hanging in the air. I leaped and swung at his back, knocking him flat and cutting into his spine. The cracking of bone shook the blade. He screamed, unable to move. I jammed my sword point through the sinew behind his ankle. He screamed, and I pierced the other one, crippling him completely. He tried to rise but could barely push himself up on his arms.

He was beaten. One more strike with my sword would shatter his neck. Widukind would be dead, the pagan rebellion would be over, and I would die a Christian hero.

Seeing him writhing on the ground, I hesitated. In that moment, a powerful blow hit me across my back, knocking me to my knees. I tried to rise but was struck again, landing flat on my stomach. I gasped, the wind knocked from me. The Wulfhednar moved in, spear tips at my throat and chest. The scar on my chest burned as if they had already pierced it.

The Walkyrie reined her stallion close. It snorted and pawed at the ground, kicking dust at me.

"Tell your King and your God to stay out of Saxony," she said, digging her heels into her mount.

Her wings flap…
Once, twice, three times
Climbing into the sky
…and the Raven soars above…

Widukind stood as if I had never hit him. His ankles were unbloodied, and his spine was strong and whole. My blade had had no effect on him. His dark rage was gone.

He took a few steps away from me. "Leave him," he said to his pack.

Grabbing the snout of his wolf hood, he pulled it low over his face and howled. The Wulfhednar answered in unison, and they evaporated into the trees like a drop of water on a red-hot iron.

I lurched to my feet, gasping, and stumbled after them. A tangle of branches closed around me, catching and holding my mantle. I unpinned the fibula, freeing myself, but immediately tripped over a vine. The bushes knotted in front of me into a thick wall. I hacked with my sword but could not cut through it.

"Fight me! Fight me!" I shouted until my voice grew hoarse and my sword was dulled and dented. My arm aching, I stopped, the haunting echo boiling inside me.

A long snapping, snarling shriek
My teeth bared
…seething

From far away
A howl answers
Another

…and another
The voice of the pack
Summoning me into the forest
I do not answer

It calls, a longer wail, more distant and isolated
Father
Calling me to his side
An aching, lonely call

"You are *not* my father, Wulfhedinn," I whispered.

Admitting Fault with Themselves

I returned to the road and searched for the monk's brown habit among the bodies of the slain soldiers. The Scola horsemen and foot soldiers lay still, not a breath of life among them. Every man had been pierced by at least two arrows and beheaded. I turned over one body, knocking the head next to it, and it rolled away. My hands went ice cold as I turned over more soldiers, fearing that I would find the monk's severed head. But I could not stop searching.

I worked my way through the Scola horsemen and the infantry. None of the riders' horses were laying injured or dead; they had all run off. The archers and the Wulfhednar had aimed precisely at the soldiers, so they could capture some of the loose horses.

The monk was not here on the road, but I smelled stale beer and goat's blood nearby. I followed the scent from into the forest. At a dozen paces, I found him cowering behind a large rock.

He dropped his seax. His face was pallid, his eyes darting back and forth, not recognizing me.

"Wolf demon!" he shrieked, trying to twist out of my grip. "My Lord God! Save me from this evil!"

"Pyttel, it is I, Tracker," I said.

He would not focus on me and continued to shriek. "—Not my time yet—not my time—"

I shook him until his arms flailed. "Look at me." I grabbed his face and pulled it close. "I am no longer a Wulfhedinn!"

His gaze met mine, and he stopped struggling, so I released him.

"Gerwulf, yes, yes—it is you." He patted my shoulders and arms as if unsure I was not an illusion. "Yes, you came back. God brought you to save me. They bounded from the woods like wild animals—and her—the Eater of Souls! She came after me!" He trembled. "With the head and wings of a raven. She chilled my soul, as if she could snatch it from me, right through my body."

"She is gone," I said in a steady tone. "They are all gone. They will not hurt you now."

"You killed them?"

"No," I said.

"You fought them all off? But there is not a drop of blood on you."

"They are gone. Nothing else matters."

Before I could stop him, he grabbed my sword from its sheath. In a snap, he had gone from a quivering coward to the clever monk—with the sharp skills of a soldier.

"No blood," he said, examining the blade, "but what have you done to it? Did use it to chop wood?"

I snatched it from him and sheathed it quickly. "Shut your mouth, monk."

He gave me a twisted smile. "You searched for me," he said. "You were worried."

"I never want to worry about you again," I snapped. "What happened to my horse?"

He scratched his crushed nose and sniggered. "That wild thing bucked and pulled me off my own horse when the attack began. She ran off."

"I should have known a monk could not hold her," I said.

He pouted. "I was an accomplished horseman in my day as a soldier," he said.

I scanned the edge of the woods for signs of the witch and her Wulfhednar, but they were gone—for now. Still, I did not lower my guard. I combed the area for crushed grass and broken brush, but the stealthy wolf warriors had left no trace. They had slipped through the landscape like snakes to make their attack and had recoiled back into thickets.

I quickly found the spot where the archers had stood. Their position was on a slight rise in the terrain, well-hidden but with a good view of the road—a perfect place to release a crippling volley of arrows onto unwary soldiers. Their restless feet had trampled a wide swath of grass a child could follow. They were peasants, not Wulfhednar.

The cunning witch was baiting me to follow their trail, but I would wait for my orders from the General. I returned to the road, thinking how he had not hesitated to leave me alone to face the wolves. At the time, I had wanted him to retreat. I had wanted to save him, to sacrifice myself—and reap the benefit myself. But it also bothered me that he had taken full advantage of it. Either way, it had been my job to protect him, and I had been presented with no choice but to try to redeem myself after failing to warn him of the attack.

"You are fretting yet again," said Pyttel. "You should have listened to me and not chased after them. The Wulfhedinn in you would have sensed this attack; the man had failed in the most human way."

I almost wanted to choke him to make him stop talking, but his eyes rolled back, and he gaped at the sky in the manner he did when God talked to him.

"My Lord, I understand," he said. "Yes, yes." He sniggered, his tongue dangling over his lips. "Be at peace, Tracker! The Lord assures me the General will not chastise you for this. No one has forgotten you returned the Holy Spear to the King. Neither the General nor the King will be so quick to find fault—not when they have so publicly favored you. They would be admitting fault with themselves." He lowered his voice and added, "Of course, what they say or do to you in private is a different matter."

"I cannot stand the sound of your voice right now, monk." I left him to return to the road. His hasty footsteps followed me like an edgy squirrel scampering through the brush.

The sound of galloping horses rose from the direction of the Lippespringe garrison. Within moments, the General burst around a bend in the road, followed closely by a dozen horsemen and a score of infantrymen running on foot. Horse Master Gallo and the shield bearers brought up the rear. The boys were armed with shields and spears. The General had summoned all the shield bearers, but it did not surprise me. He and Gallo would not hesitate to muster the youngest boys to boost their show of strength, even if it meant losing them to the Wulfhednar.

Ansgar, Heric, and the other shield bearers rode with spears poised, their faces bright with the anticipation of battle. Their helmets sank low on their heads, and their shoulders hunched under the weight of heavy mail coats.

They drove their horses past a bank of heavy brush, unmindful of the heavy cover, which could conceal Wulfhednar lying in wait. They were unaware of the rise beyond the trees, which had an unobstructed view of the road. From there, Saxon archers could hit them before they could blink. They were blind to their vulnerability. Only I knew for certain the Wulfhednar had retreated and how lucky the boys were—this time.

The shield bearers' faces darkened when they saw the headless Scola soldiers. The younger ones pulled back on the reins, shocked by the sudden certainty of danger. Ansgar and a few of the older ones slowed but continued forward.

"Keep the line!" Ansgar ordered.

The General ignored the arrow still lodged in his thigh. Spotting me, he spurred to my side. "I rode for reinforcements, but it seems the battle is over," he said.

So, he had not retreated to save his own skin. He had returned with support—and seemed relieved to see me alive.

Pyttel crossed himself. "Blessed be God you survived, General."

"They cannot kill me so easily," he said. "Devious bastards. They pelted us with arrows to knock the Scolas out of their saddles before striking with axes. Then they retreated into the shadows before I could mount a counteroffensive. They are probably watching us now."

"The Wulfhednar have retreated far into the forest," I said. "There is no sign of them nearby, but I found the place where they and their archers had waited in ambush, there to the north." I pointed. "A ridge of high ground with a clear sightline of the workers and soldiers. It is nearly impossible to see the place from the road, a perfect spot to launch an ambush."

Horse Master Gallo reined his mount toward me and curled his upper lip. "If you know so much, why did you fail to warn us of their attack, Royal Scout?"

"Tracker was fulfilling another duty for me," the General said.

Pyttel was right; he would not decry me publicly for my failure, but the deepening furrow between his brow told me we would exchange words later.

Gallo scoffed. "I am done here," he said.

"Horse Master Gallo, take half of your shield bearers and half of the foot soldiers back to the garrison," the General said. "Increase the guard at the gate and on the walls, and dispatch three extra patrols to safeguard traffic on the Hellweg to Paderborn. The other half of the infantry and shield bearers will stay here to collect the bodies for burial. We will discuss further plans upon my return."

"Yes, my lord," Gallo said.

The General glanced at the arrow in his thigh. "I will show Widukind that his pathetic little ambush has only strengthened my offensive." He ordered the remaining shield bearers and infantrymen to gather the bodies and told me to guard Pyttel. "He has much work to do now," he said.

Pyttel was stepping carefully amongst the fallen, administering last rites. Attracted by the smell of blood, ravens gathered. They circled overhead, soaring on oily black wings, and shrieked like fiends from dark places in Hell. Screeching, they dove at the bodies and attacked one another, each trying to claim the feast for themselves.

"Keep the ravens off the bodies!" Pyttel shouted to the soldiers. He chased the birds with a stick while quickening his blessings.

The noise of the screaming ravens grew so loud some soldiers put their hands over their ears. Others cowered in fear.

"They want to drink Christian blood and take the soldiers' souls to Hell," one of them said.

They had nothing to fear. None of these ravens spoke to me like the Eater of Souls did. She would not come here.

Ansgar ordered the shield bearers to stand on guard. He told the infantrymen to chase off the ravens and gather the fallen soldiers.

"The seasoned men of the infantry would make a better watch than the shield bearers," I said to the General.

He grunted in agreement. "Ansgar is trying to spare his boys the grisly task, but they must do what is best for the whole unit, not what is easiest for them. Tell Ansgar I want the shield bearers to gather the bodies. Then take his horse and patrol the length of the road to Paderborn. Make sure the Wulfhednar are nowhere near."

"Yes, General," I said.

I relayed the General's orders to Ansgar and the captain of the infantry. The captain quickly directed his foot soldiers to set a perimeter guard, but Ansgar hesitated, looking to the General. The General's iron expression did not change. Ansgar dropped his shoulders, resolved to his task, and repeated the orders to the boys. None of them moved to get off their horses. Boys, as well as men, felt safer in the saddle of a large horses— and they did not want to handle the corpses.

"Dismount!" Ansgar barked.

Heric was the first to obey, and the others followed. The next part of the General's order was more difficult for Ansgar. He glanced around, as if hoping no one would notice. Finally, he dismounted and gave me his reins, his cheeks burning red. I understood the shame he felt in handing over his mount in front of everyone, but it was a small thing. It would pass. There were far worse types of shame that could haunt a man.

"Chase those damned scavengers away," Ansgar ordered impatiently, waving his sword wildly at one, nearly hitting it.

The foot soldiers shouted and swung their weapons, scattering the birds. They did not fly far, landing in nearby branches, waiting for a chance to eat of the dead. Pyttel continued providing last rites, glancing back and forth from the ravens to me as he mumbled his prayers. I shook my head.

The Raven does not feast here.

He smiled and continued, providing the fallen with compete absolution, no matter the sins they had committed in life.

The boys loaded the mutilated remains into wagons. They moved slowly, lifting the soldiers' heads by the hair and carrying them as far away from themselves as possible. They had to hold the corpses closer, grabbing them under the arms and by the legs. No one talked as they hoisted them into the wagons while turning their heads away from the split skulls, bloodied faces, and sliced limbs. Breathing through their mouths, they swallowed hard to keep their stomachs from turning. Some of them had to drop their burdens to retch and vomit. The boys were soon blood-smeared. Heric wiped his face, spreading blood across his cheek along with the tears he was trying to wipe away.

I patrolled beyond the sight of the guards, listening, smelling, and watching for the Wulfhednar. Their scent had dispersed, and the forest remained silent. I searched for Blitz, but there was no sign of her. I hoped she had followed the road back to the garrison, but my heart told me that the spirited mare had run far away from there.

The fallen Scola horsemen were brought back to Paderborn to the palace church. The peasant foot soldiers were taken to the town church. The next day, there would be requiem Masses and burials before the bodies rotted in the heat of late summer.

The Ivory Box

General Theoderic poured a thick spot of wax onto two folded documents and stamped them with his ring. Several drops of hot wax dripped onto his hand, but he did not flinch as they cooled and hardened on his skin.

"Relay the urgency of this message to King Karl and this summons to the Saxon counts," he said, handing the dispatches to the messenger. "Count Hessi and his nobles must report to here to meet with the King within a fortnight or their titles will be forfeited."

"Yes, my lord." The messenger tucked the summons into his bag and left.

"The King will want to address this incident himself," Theoderic said. "We will prepare for his visit—and it will not be a pleasant one. He will be forced to delay other plans. His temper and his punishment will be swift if he must wait for the Saxon counts to arrive."

He stood and limped across the room. Blood dripped from his saturated breeches onto the floor. He had refused to see the physician and had cut off the arrow shaft himself. The tip was embedded deeply in his thigh, and the blood trailed him around his quarters. Leaning heavily against the table, he drank deeply from a flagon, far more than his usual sparse sips. He downed the entire thing and sat on a stool. Panting, he said, "Bring me my dagger from the fire, Gerwulf."

He called me Gerwulf, my name, my real name. My birth name sounded foreign to me, and I did not know how to react.

"God in heaven! Are you deaf?" he asked, his face paling, his forehead wet with sweat. "Bring me my dagger."

The blade was red hot from laying in the coals. The leather-wrapped handle was hot too, so I carried it with a cloth.

"Do not look at me like that," he said as he grabbed the dagger from me. "I have done this many times before."

I did not suggest he see the physician or allow me to do it. He would not listen.

He waited for the blade to cool and slashed through his breeches, exposing the wound. He pushed the tip of his blade into his thigh to make the cut. Sweat rolled off his forehead and down his face. He panted, grunted, and gritted his teeth. "Cursed Saxon bastards—" His eyes rolled back, his color grew grayer, and he dropped the dagger.

I caught him as he collapsed and lowered him to the ground. He groaned and mumbled more curses. I took the dagger, ready to cut the arrowhead out quickly.

Water...

She washes my wounds gently with water

I called out the door to the guard, "Bring me lots of water, clean water."

They gaped with dumbfounded expressions.

"One of you, go!" I ordered. "Buckets of fresh water from the well."

When he returned, I poured large amounts over the wound, the dagger, and my hands. The General stirred and passed out again. Making a quick cut to free the arrowhead, I pulled it out. He groaned and lay still. I poured more water over the wound and wrapped it tightly with linen from his bedding.

I picked him up with less effort than it normally took to lift a man. He looked frail in my arms, his robust essence soaking through the bandage with the blood. I bound more layers around the wound until the bleeding slowed and stopped.

For the first time, I saw him as the old man he was, weak with colorless lips. I thought he might not survive. He had lost a lot of blood, and he might not have the stamina he did when he was younger to fight the festering and the fever. He should have seen the physician immediately, but instead, he rallied reinforcements and returned to the ambush site. That was why he was the General.

I had little time to think more about it before he began mumbling.

"The King—the King."

He passed out and slept for several hours. At dusk, he awoke. He was pale, but there was a spark in his flinty eyes. "Is it out?"

I gave him the arrow. "Yes."

A smile dangled on the corner of his upper lip. "It will take more than this to kill me. Now, it is time to get on with things."

He moved his legs over the edge of the bed. I tried to support him, but he pushed me away with more strength than I expected. Taking several deep breaths, he rose to his feet, wobbled slightly, and limped to his desk. He deposited the arrowhead in an ivory box decorated with intricate designs of entwined dragons. It was the only ornamented thing I had seen in the General's possession. Probably a gift from the King, but it was out of place on his desk.

His eyes cleared, and the look of hardened strength returned to his face. "I have requested reinforcements from the King so work on the road can continue," he said, as if I had removed a tick from his leg instead of an arrow. "For now, we wait. It is too dangerous to proceed without more Scola horsemen to guard us."

He unrolled a map. "The King will be leaving his residence and crossing the Rhine River within the week." He pointed to the river crossing. "He planned to head south to Bavaria to finalize plans for conquest of the Huns. Those barbarians continue to raid and plunder the eastern border of Bavaria. Now the King must first detour north to Paderborn to bring our reinforcements." He traced the course with his finger. "He will also want to question the Saxon counts himself."

I studied the route. "It is not such a long diversion for a hearty rider like the King—a two-day ride on a swift horse," I said.

"He travels with a large army mustered for the Hun campaign, which will slow his progress," he said. "He will likely send the army ahead to Bavaria and ride here quickly with a light guard and our replacements. I hope he brings enough Scola horsemen to replenish those I lost to the rebels." He shook his head. "His temper fouls when good horsemen are lost, and he must delay plans for a campaign."

"You are worried he may blame you?"

He pursed his thin, pale lips. "You have a clever bold tongue when you choose to use it. The King will no sooner blame me as anyone else in his trust. He knows that the treachery lies with the Saxons, not those closest to him. It is evident now they waited to attack until you had left to burn the horse carcass. They knew you would have sensed them and warned us if you had been there."

"I should have seen it."

"*I* should have seen it," he said. "In any case, your presence may lighten the King's mood. He favors you."

"Because I returned the Holy Spear to him," I said. "Because I returned to his service after being captured by the Saxons."

When I could have stayed with them

"Because you, a Wulfhedinn, a demon, are probably the only truly honorable man in this kingdom."

Honorable?

The General ignored my puzzled look. "I sent him a report of what you learned during your captivity with the Saxon rebels, but he will have many questions for you, such as why you did not keep the wolf skin."

"I am not—"

"I know, no longer the Wulfhedinn, although that is why the King took you into his inner circle."

"The cross of God makes me more powerful than the Devil's skin."

He thought for a moment. "You did stand between me and the Wulfhednar and chase them off by yourself without the wolf skin," he mused, opening the ivory box and toying with the arrowhead. "You saved me, from the Wulfhednar and from this arrow. I will tell the King what you have done and not speak of it again, but I will never forget. It is my way."

I nodded, suspecting there were many things weighing heavily on the General after years in battle. He hid his burdens behind an impenetrable stone wall, but now a tiny bit of the mortar was cracking, allowing me a glimpse inside. A wave of gratitude washed over me like a crashing wave. Praying with gratitude to God had never felt like this.

"Thank you, my lord," I said.

I was much like the General, stowing my darkness, my anguish and shame in rock. I had tried to abandon my pain and disgrace in the chamber at the top of the Raven's Stones. I had tried to lock them there with my wolf skin and axes and all the incidents I did not want to remember. They should have stayed hidden away, but I could not keep such horrors stashed as well as the General did. He had had years more practice.

The General put the arrowhead back in the box and showed me what was inside. There were five arrowheads and four spear tips, carefully arranged from smallest to largest. Each was stained with dried blood—his blood. Had he cut them all out of his body and kept them like trophies to his strength and grit? Maybe he drew power from them as charms, or they might have been amulets against harm.

He picked up the largest arrowhead and said, "This one I cut out of my shoulder myself," he said. His facial features softened from iron to wood that was slowly softening from rot. "It was shot by my son's bow."

I wanted to touch the arrowhead, but a sharp chill shot through my arm, and I pulled away. He put it back in the box and slammed the lid shut.

"As Brother Pyttel has told me many times, I am not a man who comprehends the subtlety of God's voice," he said. "When you came here to serve the King, I began to understand. I have finally heard God clearly. He sent you to me for a reason." He limped from his desk to a chest on the other side of the room. He opened a chest and retrieved a sword. One bony index finger trembled twice as he drew it from its leather scabbard. "This will help you," he said, offering it to me. "It was my son's."

His *son's* sword?

"My son is dead to me." His voice wavered with bitterness, and his eyes probed mine briefly. He was seeking something in me.

I did not know what to do or say, so I waited for him to speak.

"He was an insolent and defiant boy," he said, holding out the sword. "He grew to become a devious traitor. I raised him to be a proud and honorable Scola horseman, and he became a giant of a man, stronger and more skilled than any other. He could have followed in my footsteps and become one of King Karl's great generals. A path of gold was laid before him. All he had to do was follow it." His voice faltered, and he had to clear his throat. "But he spat on his noble birth and all the honors he had been given. He defied my authority many times. In a rage, he shot me in the shoulder with an arrow. Then he betrayed his King—and stole the Holy Spear."

Stole the Holy Spear

My jaw dropped. I remembered the giant of a man, the leader of the three Scola thieves. The *General's* son? By luck or by God's grace, I had overheard his plans to sell the stolen Holy Spear to the Saxons. Invoking the rage and power of the wolf, I had grabbed the opportunity to redeem my sins. I had killed him and the other thieves, returning the precious holy relic to the King.

I had not known who he was, but if I had, would I have changed my course of action? No, the Wulfhedinn would have emerged and attacked and taken the spear anyway. None of that mattered now. As the killer of his son, I had no choice but to face him.

Staring into the General's iron eyes, I tried to read his intent. If he wanted revenge, why had he not killed me already? Had he waited until now for a reason? My hand rested on the pommel of my sword, ready to draw it in defense.

He could not slay a Wulfhedinn in his weakened condition. He was too cunning to be that brash, but he might call his guards and—

"Take the sword, Tracker," he said.

I hesitated, watching the door, expecting his guards to burst in.

"My own son disgraced himself and me," he said. "My wife has passed, and I have no other family. I am too old to have another. My son's sword is yours. Wield it with the honor he never had." He blinked several times. Was he trying to blink away tears?

The heavy burden of grief and shame he carried was the same as mine. He had hewn through the many layers of stone that he had built around his son's dishonor to present his sword to me. He was offering an exchange of sorts, accepting me in place of the son he had lost—long before I killed him.

I was thinking his thoughts and feeling his emotions. Why? I often perceived the thoughts and emotions of others. I anticipated their motivations and actions, so I could attack them before they could hurt me. It was a skill I had perfected, but this was different.

The sword rested in his hands between us. I reached for it slowly, and as soon as my fingers touched the hilt, it seemed right to do so.

I pulled it from its sheath. The pommel was plainer than that of the sword the King had given me, but I did not care. It was the heftiest weapon I had ever handled, heavier than my long axe had been. The blade was as fine as the King's sword, but different. The edges were not honed sharply, and it lay far heavier in my grasp. It was a bone crusher—more of an iron club with a pointed tip than an elegant cutting blade. In the hands of someone strong enough to wield it, a single blow could shatter a hip and tear a large hole in the flesh from the impact. It quickly became an extension of my arm, a part of me.

"Thank you, my lord," I said, sheathing it. I hung the sheath on my belt and liked the weight of it on my hip.

The General patted my shoulder. Had he ever come this close to embracing another? Had I? I trusted his brief touch. It connected me to him with a deep sense of obligation that was greater than the fealty and duty I owed the King. This was a different type of gift, and there was no way to repay it. I would have to spend a lifetime trying.

"Thank you, my lord," I said.

His face returned to stone, as if nothing had changed.

One of Them

The tolling of bells echoed through the palace. It beckoned us with sorrowful tones to the requiem Mass for the slain soldiers. The General walked slowly, trying to suppress his limp, but he could not hide his clenched jaw and the pallor in his face. It was subtle, but I saw his pain. I almost asked him about it, but it was better to let him bear it in his own way.

The chanting of monks joined the ominous ringing of the bells as we walked through the huge door of the church. A woeful song resonated on the stone walls. I cringed at their hallowed singing. The Latin words were a mystery to most, a magical chorus to invoke God, but I understood them. From my days in the monastery, I knew the translation, but I suffered their real meaning on my scarred back.

You have been flogged
Scourged deeply, many times

Flesh torn
Hanging like red ribbons

Her gentle finger traces the ridged scars on my back
Who did this to you?

…God

I had avoided going to Mass since my return to Paderborn. I had often lingered in the forest, patrolling until regular Masses were over, dodging the desolate sounds of bells and chanting. That day, I could not elude it; everyone was expected at the requiem for the Scola horsemen.

As we took our places in the front of the church, I tried to close my ears to the sounds.

The coffins of the horsemen were lined up by the altar. I pictured the headless bodies inside. Would God accept them in heaven? Were the sins of repentant soldiers and killers ever truly forgiven?

I shifted like a restless child as the bishop prayed in Latin. I wished I were somewhere else, anywhere else. I wanted it to be over, to flee into the woods. I made the sign of the cross, hoping it would ease the tightening of my chest. It was slowly squeezing the breath out of me. I gasped, sweat running down my neck. I wanted to run from this place, but I could not do such a thing, not as the King's Royal Scout and Huntsman, not as the man who carried the sword of the General's son.

I pulled at the collar of my tunic, reminding myself of Pyttel's guidance. He had told me it would take time to feel the grace of God. I had to be patient, but I was tired of waiting. I had won back my soul and had earned absolution. How long it would take to be at peace? I could wall off the shame of my sins and suppress the wolf creature, but would I ever conquer its rage?

Wear the skin of the wolf in shame
Let it mark you
A captive of your God and your King
…knowing you will forever be damned by them
Never one of them

The witch's words came from nowhere, as if spoken aloud, as if she stood next to me. Something caught in my throat, smothering me. I jerked my head around in panic, but I did not see her or the Raven in the church. The General's cool presence warmed me. I dropped my hand to my side, to his son's sword. Clinging to the pommel like a lifeline, I mouthed the words to prayers and locked out the monks' chanting.

After it was finally over, the coffins of the Scola horsemen were loaded into carts to make their last journey back to their estates. The wooden boxes rattled as they rolled through town. There was no glory in being carried like children or feeble old men in carts. They never would have ridden this way in life.

Some of the infantrymen were taken back to their villages for burial. Those without means were hauled to a mass grave at the far end of the churchyard. All morning, the gravediggers had worked, digging the pit. The sound of shovels jamming against dirt and rock had rung through town, drawing me there.

A couple of dozen ravens had gathered, attracted by the smell of exposed corpses. They perched on the roof of the church and in nearby trees, cackling and anxious to feed. I scanned each one, but they were merely common ravens.

A young woman stood at the edge of the pit. Her mantle was pulled over her head, shadowing her face as she watched the scavengers. She shivered and pulled the filthy, bloodstained material tightly around her shoulders.

"Have you come to keep watch too?" she asked. Her voice was small, like a child's, and her accent was not Frankish—it was Saxon.

"I do not know why I came," I said.

"The others have said their prayers and their goodbyes," she said. "They cannot bear to watch the gravediggers, but someone has to stay. Someone has to make sure the bodies are buried deep enough so the ravens cannot peck at them."

Several of the black scavengers grew bold and landed at the edge of the pit. The girl grabbed a stick and chased them. "Be off with you!" she screamed.

The ravens scattered, flying to perch on the church roof. They ruffled their feathers, watching, waiting for their chance to feast.

The girl's hood fell back, and I recognized her from somewhere. Her face was marred by a crooked nose and a sunken cheek from a severe beating or an accident. She wiped tears from her crushed cheek and gazed at me. Her mouth fell open, and she stepped back, pulling her mantle tightly around her. "Are you him?" she asked.

"I am Tracker, the King's Royal Scout and Huntsman."

"You are him!" she cried. "The wolf demon!"

My gut twisted into a knot. Who was this girl?

"From that night in the ravine," she said. "You sliced off his cullions and hacked him to death—the soldier who violated me." She rubbed her runny broken nose on her sleeve. "You gave me his cloak to cover myself."

Lying atop the girl
The soldier rams her
Punches her bloodied face
Rams her again
…and again

I glanced around, relieved no one had been nearby to over-hear her. I struggled to say something, to deny it, but I could not.

"Why would the Royal Huntsman kill a soldier to save a Saxon slave?" she asked.

A slave. Her frayed tunic blew over bare feet, standing on the edge of a pit full of dead paupers. Was there a brother, father, or husband lying among the twisted corpses below? Would she have anyone or anything now?

She pulled the mantle over her face. "I carry his child and will bear his bastard," she said. "The priest says I brought this disgrace upon myself. I deserve this broken face—and worse after death."

Her words were soaked in shame, paining me as if her dis-honor was my own.

"Talk with Brother Pyttel," I said. "He can help you."

She scoffed. "The King's monk? A court monk would never receive someone such as me."

I wanted to help her, but I was unsure why. Maybe I wanted her pain to stop, or maybe I thought it would erase the bloody memory for me. I spoke before I could stop myself. "I can take you to him."

She laughed, a long deep belly laugh. "You? The demon who serves a Christian King? And your monk, he is no different. He makes blood sacrifice to the pagan gods in secret."

How would she know such things?

She stepped so close to me I could smell her body.

Sweet musk and hawthorn

"Have you not learned anything from the Raven?" she asked. "You are not one of them."

She soars overhead
On black wing
...floating on the smell of death
Rising from the pit

The mantle fell, and she stood before me, glossy black hair and eyes the color of the midsummer sky.

The witch of the Raven's Stones
The Walkyrie
The Raven
Vala

My throat tightened. She could *not* be here. She was not real. But I could not deny how her breasts rose and fell as she breathed. The sun moved from behind a cloud, and she shaded herself from the glare with one hand. She squinted, small lines forming on her face.

No. She could not be standing here—could not.

Enchantment
Playing with my mind
Deceiver

I wanted to touch her to be sure. Would my hand pass through her like a ghost or would it stop to caress the alluring warmth of her flesh?

"How did you—?" Words failed me. I wanted to draw my sword against her, but my hand hung at my side as if dismembered from my body.

She laughed. "Do you truly believe soldiers and a palisade wall can keep me out? You cannot hide from the Raven here."

"Where is the slave girl?" I demanded.

She moved closer. "I am her, and she is you."

I stepped back, peering around. The gravediggers were busy throwing bodies into the pit and covering them with chalk and dirt. No one had noticed her.

"You called upon the wolf and killed a Frankish soldier to save a Saxon slave," she said. "She is here, where you stand, within your soul. She is the embodiment of your true honor, the honor of Wulfhedinn blood flowing in your veins."

She was trying to mystify me with her words and seduce me with her body. She wanted to pull me back into Hell, to invoke the Wulfhedinn in me and make me one of her pack. She had succeeded for a brief time when holding me captive at the Raven's Stones, but she would not prevail against my will again. I had fought for my soul and won it, and I would not fall captive to her.

"Witch!" I seethed. "Have you brought Widukind and the Wulfhednar into Paderborn too?"

She knotted her dark brows. "Wolves must breach the walls to get in," she said sharply. "They are not the Walkyrie, Chooser of the Living and the Slain. Walls cannot stop me."

"You do not frighten me, witch," I said.

"I did not come to scare you. I came to remind you, to re-tell the tale of Midsummer—the day of your great joy when you descended from the great tower. The day you emerged from death into your new life—the day you loved me as Vala."

She moved closer, her scent overpowering me.

Sweet musk and hawthorn

I stepped away but could not escape it.

She licked her lips. "I spilled my blood and that of the Wul-fhednar. I mixed it together with yours, joining Walkyrie, you, and the Wulfhednar pack," she said. "I chose you, and you are bound to me, to the pack, by blood, and by will—if it be your will."

"No!" I shouted, but no sound came from my throat. The gravediggers did not stop their work to look at us. I was alone in fighting her power.

Her eyes softened like those of a mortal woman. "Your people need you," she pleaded. "Widukind, your father, needs you—" She licked her lips. "—*I* need you. I hunger, and only you can feed me, Gerwulf."

She took my face in her hands and drew my lips toward hers. For a moment, I surrendered to her.

Sweet musk and hawthorn

I pulled away, trying to wipe away the taste of her. "I am no longer your prisoner to bend to your will!"

She scowled, crossing her arms. "You think that your title and your Frankish sword makes you one of them?"

My hand fell to the hilt of my sword. "Every Frankish man

who sees this blade wishes it were his and envies the favor the General has given me."

"Your general, your King, and your God will betray you in the end," she said. "You will never be the son of a Frankish general. You cannot deny your blood, Wulfhedinn, son of Widukind."

"Liar! Deceiver!" I said, drawing my sword. "You will never take me."

She touched my wrist and smiled. "I already have."

The Walkyrie unfurled sleek black wings and rose on the breeze. She flew out of the graveyard, leaving the taste of the woman on my lips.

Under Arrest

The General limped on his injured leg in a foul mood. With every painful step, he grew more cross. It was raining again, a hard pounding rain that delayed work on the road. He grumbled about everything. He watched the rain from his window, cussing every drop and muttering about the setbacks on the road. He bemoaned the Scola soldiers and infantry he had lost and snapped at every servant and guardsman who entered his quarters. He complained much about how long the Saxon counts were taking to report to him.

Clearly, his leg wound irritated him the most. It was healing too slowly for his liking, but fortune was with him. It did not stink of festering, and he did not suffer a fever, even though he had not changed the dressing. He was refusing to acknowledge the injury—it reminded him that his body did not mend itself as quickly as it had in younger days.

"You should wash the wound every day with fresh water and put on a clean dressing," I said. "It will heal faster."

The corner of his drooping eyelid twitched. "Do not talk to me like I am an invalid," he snapped.

He loathed reminders of his age, of his weakness. His gaze remained hard, like ice, although his vision was fading, and his skin was beginning to hang loosely from his shrinking muscles.

I resisted the urge to snap back at him, but I was tired of it. He had no reason to throw his bad temper at me. He would have been killed in the ambush if not for me, and he might have died from the arrow if I had not taken it out and cared for him.

"Do not talk to the Saxon counts when they arrive," he said. "Do not tell them about the rebels at the Raven's Stones." He repeated it countless times while we awaited their arrival. His repetitiveness was making him sound like a doddering old man.

"I have no desire to speak with Saxons," I replied many times.

"Where are they?" he grumbled as he paced incessantly in his quarters. "If the King arrives first and must wait for them, they will wish they had not come at all."

Fortune was with Count Hessi; he and his entourage of half a dozen high-ranking Saxons arrived at the gates before the King did. His personal guard was ordered to make camp outside the town walls, and he and his nobles were taken to the General. Guards were posted in the room and outside the door.

The count's fur-trimmed mantle and silk tunic were soaked. He looked as uncomfortable and unhappy as a cat that had been thrown into a river. A large silver cross lay on his chest, glistening with raindrops. His nobles also wore their crosses obediently. They were dressed less ostentatiously, but they were as wet and as miserable as he was.

Hessi and his nobles flung off their wet mantles and stood close to the fire, trying to dry themselves. Hessi's gaze swept over the heavy guard and fell on me. I scowled at him. He had always appeared loyal to the King, but I did not trust the words pouring like melted butter from his thin lips. Other Saxon nobles had accused him of trading the freedom and souls of all Saxons for Frankish wealth and titles. I wondered what he knew about me and my captivity at the Raven's Stones. Did he know Widukind was my father?

"Are we not entitled to the hospitality of the King's palace?" he said, flicking the tip of his large nose. His nobles nodded. "We have ridden a long way in the rain to answer the King's summons."

"You will dry soon enough," the General said.

Hessi rubbed his hands together and held them near the fire. "I am not accustomed to leaving my own soldiers outside city walls."

"You will be well guarded," the General said without inviting him to sit.

"Indeed." Hessi scowled at the guards. Spotting the flagon of beer on the General's table, he licked his lips.

"The King will arrive in a day or two," the General said without pause to offer the customary refreshment. "You will remain in your quarters until he summons you."

Hessi pursed his lips. "What is the meaning of this summons, and why have our titles been threatened? I have had to delay important matters at my own estates to attend to the King. I deserve some explanation."

"You will not be attending the King but answering to him," the General said. "Until he arrives and is ready for an audience, you and your nobles will be confined to your quarters."

"We are under arrest?"

"I could have you locked in, but that will not be necessary," said the General with a flat, calculating tone. "Your son is living in the comfort and honored care of the King's household, is he not? I do not need to remind you of the terms of such fostering. I hear the boy is particularly sensitive, a weak fighter but bright and well versed in Latin. He could have a great future in court as a scholar, or he could be sent on campaign as a foot soldier without armor or shoes. The choice is yours, Count Hessi."

Hessi's face reddened. "We shall retire to our quarters, but the King will hear of this insult." He turned on his heel.

"Oh, the King is aware."

God Would Find Fault

King Karl arrived at the palace at Paderborn the next day with his personal guard and several dozen Scola horsemen. They rode through the muddy courtyard with haste, without acknowledging his nobles who stood the rain to greet him. The King's brilliant blue mantle was wet and splashed with dirt. His face was drawn, lacking the jovial expression he could wield so well. He clutched the Holy Spear in a tight fist like a weapon, not a precious relic. Glowing with a formidable, angry power, the spear drew the awe of everyone in the courtyard. I could not tell if its force flowed from the King or from God Himself—both were rightly furious about the rebel ambush. There would be no merriment or lavish feast during this visit.

The groom took the King's horse. He immediately called the General to his quarters, where they met privately for hours.

I waited to be summoned in my room. Would the General try to blame me for the disastrous ambush? He had taken fault with himself for sending me away to get rid of the nithing horse. Under royal pressure, he might shift responsibility to me for failing to warn him of the attack—or not.

Pyttel had assured me that neither the General nor the King will be quick to find fault with me. I latched onto Pyttel's words, and thought of the Holy Spear. I had heard that it had brought God's blessing to the King during his summer campaigns in the west. He would not have had it without me. My hand grasped the pommel of the sword the General had given me—an honor setting me above all the others. I locked my jaw and refused to concede failure to them.

It was late in the day before I was called to see the King. Surprisingly, he and the General were drinking and laughing. At once, I felt more at ease.

The guard announced me formally. "My King, I present Tracker, Royal Scout and Huntsman."

The King took another drink and slammed his cup before answering. "I know who he is." His mood had darkened quickly. After the guard left, the King leaned back in his chair and said, "Remove your tunic and shirt."

I did not the sound of his order.

"Do as your King commands, Royal Scout," the General said.

I unbuckled my sword belt and undressed, dropping everything on the ground, including my breeches. The King scrutinized the long, jagged scars on my arm and leg where the severed muscles had grown together in a mismatched manner. He stared the longest at the healed gash on my belly. He put his fist into the wedge-shaped hole and ran his fingers over the mutilated texture. He was judging me by my wounds, weighing my character, my loyalty. I *wanted* him to touch them, to linger in the depth of my loyalty in a way words could not explain.

"A mortal wound," he said, "healed by the grace of God."

He embraced me abruptly, his arms as strong as a bear's. He patted me heartily on the back and handed me my breeches. "General Theoderic has told me about your ordeal with the heathens, but I had to see for myself," he said as I dressed. He gestured to a seat at his table. "I am most glad you survived and returned, Gerwulf—Wulfhedinn."

I stopped in my tracks, unsure how to respond. Calling me Gerwulf in front of the General could mean only one thing—the King thought I had revealed my identity him.

"I did not tell him," I said.

"You did not have to," the King said. "The General has always known, but your identity is to remain a secret between the three of us and Brother Pyttel."

"Yes, my King," I said.

He poured more wine for himself and passed the flagon to me. "The General tells me he had sent you to destroy another nithing horse when the rebel attack occurred," he said.

"Yes, my—"

"He also says you do not wear the wolf skin and that you left it with the heathens."

"I am no longer Wulfhedinn. I serve my King and my God."

He took another drink. "You would serve me better with it, but we will speak to this later. I understand that every Frankish worker fled the ambush and returned safely to the Lippespringe garrison. They were armed with tools, not swords. The wolf warriors could have cut them down if they had chosen. Why do you think they let them go?"

"Peasants might be more useful to the rebel cause alive than dead," I said.

The King smiled, as if he had been testing me, and I had given him the correct answer. The smile was short-lived. "The peasants are spreading more rumors and fear of the Wulfhednar," he said. "Half the kingdom east of the Rhine will hear of it by the week's end. It will make it more difficult for my nobles to muster the peasants for the road and the infantry. Worst of all, the Saxon workers who claimed to be loyal betrayed their oaths and turned on my soldiers."

"They thought they were fleeing to the winning side," I said.

The King slammed his dagger into the table, upsetting the wine cups. "They thought wrong!" he bellowed. "I will crush them, and their Wulfhednar leaders will plead for death before this is over."

"Their tactics are more dangerous than the demons they conjure," the General said. "Widukind led a highly organized ambush requiring discipline and the training of expert archers. Gerwulf saw them preparing at the Externsteine."

"Were Count Hessi or any of his nobles conspiring with Widukind there?" the King asked.

"Difficult to tell," I said. "I was locked high above the ground in a tower. From what I could see, most of the rebels, except the Wulfhednar, appeared to be free farmer peasants."

"Hessi and the other nobles like him are not fool enough to openly side with the rebels," said the General. "They have been given too much to lose."

The King's cheeks flushed. "But they have done *nothing* to stop the rebels," he said. "They are walking a razor-sharp edge of a sword between the rebels and their King. One misstep and I will ensure it splits their cullions!" He pounded the table. "And they *will* answer to me for this calamity."

"In any case," the General said, "building a road through the Teutoburg Forest will require far more military protection. Using more soldiers from Paderborn and the Lippespringe garrison will compromise security in those places. The only source of new riders we have at hand is Gallo's shield bearers."

"I will replace some of your Scola with the riders I brought," said the King, "but I need to replenish them for my campaign against the Huns in the east. Have Horse Master Gallo report to me on the training progress of the shield bearers. I need them to be named Scola—now."

General Theoderic scratched his chin. "I have overseen Horse Master Gallo's training. Many of the boys are not ready yet. They do not have sufficient experience in combat and need another season or two of attending Scola horsemen before they will be a fighting asset."

"Most are too young," I said.

"Nonsense!" the King said. "One of my own sons, Prince Pepin, has fought valiantly in several battles. He is younger than many of Gallo's shield bearers—and he is a hunchback, no less. Boys become men when they are needed to do so."

"Yes, but they should be spread out among the armies," said the General, "No single commander can contend with too many unseasoned soldiers."

"Agreed," the King mused. "I will give them more time for training, but tell Horse Master Gallo to ready them. They will be summoned soon."

"Yes, my King," the General said.

The King turned his attention to me. "Now, tell me everything you learned about the Wulfhednar and their witch during your captivity."

I told him no more, and no less, than I had told the General. He listened to every word, watching my face and manner for signs of deceit, but I was an expert at concealing things best kept secret. I would never reveal Widukind as my father or that the Walkyrie had initiated me into the Wulfhednar pack.

When I had finished my story, the King said, "There are hundreds of wolf skins in the storehouse outside the palace. Find a suitable one and wear it when on patrol. Do not hesitate to call upon the wolf to fulfill your duties as Royal Scout."

He was not giving me a choice. I almost blurted out that he had no idea what I had endured to leave the wolf skin behind and return to his service. I could have stayed with them. They *wanted* me.

From deep within my chest
The wolf rises
A low growl
Aching to howl

He grinned and smoothed his long moustache. "It's good to hear the wolf's snarl and see the rage in your eyes," he said. "I need the demon. Summon it and do not worry. The burden of it will be on my soul."

I wanted to tell him that he did not understand the anguish of that burden, but he was too arrogant to believe God would punish him. God be damned. If the King wanted a devil, he would have it. I no longer had to deny it.

"I will do as you order, My King," I said.

This time I would become the Wulfhedinn and use it to my advantage—not his.

The Prophecy

The next day, the King sent guards to escort Count Hessi and the other Saxon nobles to a formal audience in the great hall. Pyttel was called to act as scribe to record the meeting, and every Scola soldier, noble, and well-to-do freeman in the town was summoned to attend.

General Theoderic and I waited in an antechamber with the King until everyone had assembled. We were soon joined by Horse Master Gallo. He looked down his nose, making it clear he was displeased to attend the King with me.

The crowd members bowed to the King and knelt, crossing themselves in reverence to the Holy Spear. He climbed the steps and sat upon the marble throne. General Theoderic took his place to his right. Gallo and I stood to the left.

"Bring in the Saxon counts," the King said.

The guards escorted the counts into the hall, and the massive oak doors slammed shut behind them. The King was succeeding in making the Saxon nobles small and insignificant in his cavernous hall.

Hessi and his nobles bowed low. Their faces were tight with worry after days of captivity, but Hessi had the arrogance to wear a gold brooch that was finer than the King's best. The King scowled, white knuckles gripping the Holy Spear. The hall was so quiet, I heard a mouse scamper across the floor.

I worried that Hessi might know Widukind was my father, but the concern quickly passed. He would have said something about it to the General by now. He was no simpleton; he would have traded the information for more favor.

General Theoderic spoke. "Come forward, Count Hessi, so you and your nobles may address the King directly."

They took several steps closer to the dais.

The General continued, "Several days ago, Scola horsemen and infantry who were protecting the Hellweg were ambushed. It was an unprovoked attack by a band of Saxons that included the Wulfhednar, the so-called wolf warriors. Count Hessi, what do you know of it?"

"I did hear of this unfortunate incident," he said.

"When?"

"There was some talk, but there are always rumors of spirits and monsters in the forest—mere peasant gossip."

The General's icy gaze never left Hessi. "Your peasants must have had contact with the rebels to hear such talk."

"My lord, falsehoods and babble spreads like lice among the rustics," he replied. "Most of it stems from drunkenness and ignorance of our Lord Jesus Christ."

"And who do your 'rustics' say led the attack?"

"They talk of the rebel Widukind, of course."

"Of course," the General said.

The King's face was flushing as he listened to the exchange.

Hessi rubbed his pointy nose nervously. "I have spies who have been keeping records on my people's activities and their attendance at church," he said. "I assure you my tribes in East-phalia are not worshipping the old gods and joining the rebellion. They remain loyal to King Karl and are faithful Christians. The rebels are coming from Widukind's lands in Westphalia."

"You are either a liar or an inept lord who is unable to keep a firm grip on his people and his administration," the General said coolly. "We know free peasants from your lands have joined the rebellion."

Hessi crossed his arms over his chest. "A lie, likely spread by other Saxon nobles who conspire with Widukind and want to shift the blame to me. Count Sidag has allied with the rebels; there must be others too."

The General's eyes narrowed, like a predator about to corner his prey. "There are other problems in your administration, Count Hessi. The priests in Eastphalia report your people have fallen behind on paying the church tithe."

"I oversee the ledger myself and see that the tithes are being paid. If the King's treasury is not receiving the money, you should question your priests."

Several people in the crowd gasped at the insult to the priests. The General let Hessi's words hang themselves in the air for a moment.

The General continued, "At the assembly in early summer, the King had charged you and your noble kin with bringing in the rebel Widukind. You swore allegiance to King Karl and vowed to fulfill this and other duties. You were to administer your estates, and ensure the peasants became good Christians and paid the church tithe. In exchange, the King gave you high-ranking titles and control over your lands. You have fulfilled none of these obligations."

Hessi retorted defensively, "After the general assembly, the Eastphalian nobles and I mustered a large force of our best trained soldiers to track down Widukind. I have not heard reports from them for some weeks now, and I am afraid they have been attacked and killed by the rebels, but—"

The General raised his voice over Hessi's. "Why were you not riding at the head of this force you sent to track him? You have failed to find Widukind, and now his strength is growing. Our reports say he has been able to recruit and train rebels from all over Saxony, including your territories in Eastphalia."

Hessi ran his fingers through his beard and cleared his throat. "But, my King, I assure you—"

The King jumped from his throne. "I have heard enough!" His voice boomed across the hall. "Count Hessi, you will provide several companies of fully armed infantrymen and summon twenty of your best horsemen to replace those I have lost to the rebels. Each of your lords will provide a dozen more."

"My King, that would be over one hundred riders and several hundred foot soldiers!" He covered his mouth, as if he wished he had kept it shut.

The King responded quickly. "And you will remain in the General's keeping under guard until every soldier has reported for duty."

Hessi's lips moved, but he held his tongue.

One of Hessi's nobles stepped forward, a finger trembling with trepidation. "My King, I am Lord Engel. I oversee many of Count Hessi's estates and have closer contact with the free peasants than he has. I have heard many things—things I cannot verify."

The King sat. "Come forward, Lord Engel, and speak."

He cleared his throat, hesitating. "They say the Walkyrie flies again."

Another Saxon noble stepped forward. "She is the herald of Wodan!"

"The Eater of Souls!" said one of the Frankish courtiers in the crowd. A restless murmur rolled through the hall like a wave.

Hessi could not control himself any longer. "Yes, yes, we have all heard of this witch, who allegedly summons wolf devils against good Christians. Every village has a senile old woman babbling superstitious nonsense. None of what they say are of consequence."

The King slammed the Holy Spear on the dais. "I will be the judge of that!"

Hessi and the other Saxon lords shifted backward on their heels.

"What else can you tell us, Lord Engel?" the General asked.

He shifted nervously. "She flies with the black wings of the Raven, carrying the chosen ones to join Wodan in Walhalla. With her, the Wulfhednar are undefeatable, for there is no death for the wolf warrior, only honor in the afterlife."

"Hessi, why have you not told us of this?" the King bellowed.

Hessi lowered his head. "My King, I did not—"

Lord Engel interrupted. "—and there is more," he said. "They talk of a prophecy—a special child who will be born in the spring of next year. A descendant of Wodan, a redeemer who will bring the wrath of the old gods down upon all Christians."

Another wave of unrest stirred the crowd.

"Silence!" ordered the King. When the room had quieted, he said, "This will be dealt with quickly. Where can the mother of this child be found?"

"At the Raven's Stones," Lord Engel said. "They say the Walkyrie is with child."

Any One of Them

The Walkyrie is with child.

The words passed through my ears, floating through my mind, waiting for someone to say something to make sense of them.

"Who is the father of this demon seed?" the King asked Lord Engel.

"No one knows for certain," he said. "The woman is the Devil's whore—she mates with all of the wolf warriors. Any one of them could be the father, but they say she chose the strongest of them to sire the child—"

"Widukind," the King said with certainty.

"That is the rumor, but I cannot verify the truth of it."

The King smoothed his long moustache, thinking. After several long moments, he called for his guard. "Take Count Hessi and the rest of his nobles back to their quarters, where they will remain. In the morning, Lord Engel will be allowed to return to his lands as long as he relays any more information he hears to me—and I expect to hear a lot."

Several guards armed with spears surrounded Hessi and the other Saxons.

"My King," pleaded Hessi. "Truly, this is unnecessary."

The King waved his hand at the captain of the guard, who smacked Count Hessi across the face so hard he fell. The count held his cheek, burning red with humiliation, but he did not attempt to rise. None of the other Saxons protested or moved to help Hessi.

"Get him away from me," the King ordered, "before I arrest his son too."

The guards dragged Hessi to his feet and escorted him and the other Saxons out of the great hall.

The next morning, the King left Paderborn to rejoin his campaign against the Huns. Lord Engel was allowed to return to Eastphalia, but Hessi and the other Saxon nobles remained under arrest. They quickly dispatched messengers to muster the required horsemen and infantrymen needed to buy their freedom.

As ordered by the King, I chose a new wolf skin from the storehouse. I ran my fingers through the black fur, mustering the gall to wear it. I had tried and failed to leave the Wulfhedinn behind, but I had been able to control it since returning from the heathens. If I donned another wolf skin, would the demon command me? Did it matter? My King demanded it, and I could not deny his order. I would give it to him, and I would not fear it. *I* would command the Wulfhedinn.

I threw the hide over my shoulders and was relieved it did not immediately summon the wolf inside. I headed out on my daily patrol between Paderborn and the Lippespringe garrison. The wolf skin was heavier than my wool mantle, and it stank of wet fur, like my own wolf skin would have done in the rain. The smell was vaguely comforting. I preferred it—and the foul weather—to keeping company with the General and his foul mood.

Within two weeks, the Saxon soldiers arrived, and Hessi and his nobles were released. They departed in the pouring rain.

Standing at his window, the General stroked his chin as he watched them leave. "Good riddance," he murmured.

He continued to gaze out the window, barely acknowledging my routine morning report. Nothing had changed—more rain, more mud, and no sign of the rebels.

A rider interrupted me with an urgent dispatch from the King. General Theoderic's jaw tightened as he broke the seal on the message. Messengers who had ridden all night rarely brought good news. The General read it silently, the web of lines deepening on his face. He reread it several times. Finally, he handed it to me.

"Slav tribesmen are raiding our lands in Saxony on the eastern borderlands. Horse Master Gallo will immediately assemble a contingent of Scola riders from the Rhineland Franks. Gallo will also promote as many of the Paderborn shield bearers as possible to Scola status. Horse Master Gallo will take half the riders with him on the campaign, and the other half will remain with General Theoderic at Paderborn."

"Gallo will ride with inexperienced warriors—who hate him," I said.

"Those who are worthy will rise to the challenge," the General said, but he did not sound convinced.

I continued reading.

"Master Gallo will take command of his Scola riders and a company of loyal Saxon infantry coming from Eastphalia. His force will join with those of Count Hessi and his Saxon archers, as well as General Worad, Count of the Palace. They will all ride under the command of Chamberlain Adalgis.

"It is of vital importance we repress the temerity of the contumacious Slavs quickly. We must demonstrate to the Saxons that their new king will defend those who are loyal to God and the Frankish crown. Reports say the Slavs are poorly armed and disorganized. I anticipate immediate, decisive action will quickly drive the Slav barbarians out from Saxony.

"General Theoderic will remain at Paderborn and continue clearing the Hellweg and preparing to attack the rebel-held Externsteine. It is imperative Paderborn and the Lippespringe garrison remain firmly occupied and are not left vulnerable to rebel Saxon attacks during the mission against the Slavs."

I was disappointed the King had not sent for me to scout in the campaign. It would have been easier to go far to the east than to stay here, but the idea quickly passed. There was no place I could hide from the Eater of Souls, even in the distant land of the Slavs. I could not run from her. The only way to lose her forever was to destroy Widukind, the Wulfhednar, and all they represented.

I dropped the dispatch on the General's desk. I would also have to destroy her and her child as well.

Was it the child of Widukind? Could it be *mine*?

I covered my eyes with my hands, burying the idea like a dog kicking dirt over its own shit. They said she was the Devil's whore and mates with all the wolf demons. Any one of them could be the father. Any one of them—

"Is your head ailing you?" the General asked.

I dropped my hands, welcoming his interruption. "No."

"Do not fret over the King's orders," he said. "We must stay here, but we will see action soon enough." He tapped his fingers on the dispatch. "I do not like the smell of this. The rebel Saxons will hear the King has sent many of his troops to the eastern frontier and may take the opportunity to attack us. We must be prepared. Your scouting will be more vital than ever."

"Yes, General."

Trying to Save Face

Word of the Slav campaign spread rapidly. By the next day, everyone in the Paderborn streets was talking about it. In a quick ceremony that night, most of the shield bearers were granted positions as Scola horsemen. Within two days, they set out with the Horse Master for their first real campaign as fighting men. The entire population of the town came out to cheer as they paraded through the streets. I did not go to bid them farewell, convincing myself that Ansgar and little Heric would not miss me.

Instead, I slipped out of the palace before dawn, disappearing into the forest under the guise of the wolf skin. It had stopped raining overnight, and there was much I needed to do. Over the next few days, I marked a new route around the swamp. The wet area had grown larger since the recent rains, and I had to detour farther to find solid ground. Despite this, the road crews made quick progress on clearing the forest to make a passable road. They got halfway around the swamp within several days, and General Theoderic's mood lightened.

The days grew shorter as summer passed into fall. I did not sense the presence of the rebels or the Raven and had to reminded myself to stay vigilant. It had been quiet for too long in the forest. They were waiting for us to become complacent and let down our guard. They would attack soon, before winter was upon us.

I reported every night to the General and listened to his plans for the next day. He agreed that the rebels would likely attack soon, but he did not want to send me farther into the forest to hunt for signs of the Wulfhednar.

"I want you to stay within this area." He moved his finger around a small spot on the map. "Close enough to alert us of attack."

We were interrupted by his guard. "Excuse the intrusion, General Theoderic, but there is a noble outside who demands to see you immediately. He says he is a Saxon count who has urgent news."

It was Count Hessi, but I barely recognized him. His fine saffron mantle was splattered with mud and the hem had torn. His face was tight with apprehension instead of its typical haughtiness.

The General lowered the map and scrutinized his disheveled appearance. "You are supposed to be joining with Chamberlain Adalgis and his forces to fight the Sorbs with your archers."

"I come with news of the rebellion," he said. "Widukind is rallying a large group of rebels to the east of the Teutoburg Forest. My archers have all deserted me and joined him." He rubbed his neck nervously. "This is no small disturbance of rabble. It is a large, well-organized revolt."

The General cracked his knuckles, staring at Hessi. "How large?"

"Several thousand. They have established a fortified stronghold on the top of a plateau in the Süntel Hills. They are laying preparations for open battle and to defend a siege, if necessary."

The General unrolled a map. "Show me."

Hesse pointed to the spot. "It is north of here, up the Weser River Valley. They have built a fortress on a strip of high ground called the Hohenstein Plateau. It is surrounded by steep cliffs and valleys."

"Where is the access point?" asked Theoderic.

"There is a narrow strip of relatively level ground to the southeast of the fortress. It is the most viable place for a force of Scola horsemen to launch an attack. It is guarded by an encampment of Saxon infantry, but you outnumber them three to one. A charge of Scola horsemen could easily break their line."

"Is there another route to the top of the plateau?"

"There is a gully that runs from the Weser River to the western side of it." He traced the route with his finger. "But the terrain is more difficult."

Hessi's eager manner raised my suspicion. "Why would you know so much about it?"

He rubbed his pointy nose. "When my archers deserted, I sent my scouts to follow them. Only one of them returned alive to tell me of the Saxon's plans, and I would trust with my life. Send the Royal Scout to confirm my report if you do not trust me. He will see what is happening."

With narrowed eyes, the General had been analyzing every gesture Hessi made for signs of deception. "Yes, that is a good idea, Count Hessi," he said.

The General never told anyone he had a good idea. He dismissed the count abruptly and sent a rider to carry the news to the King.

"Hessi is trying to save face," I said, "and as much of the King's favor as he can salvage."

"I do not trust him either," he said, "but mark my words—King Karl will order us to march against this uprising. We must be ready to leave the moment his order arrives. I will send other scouts to spy on the rebel stronghold. The rebels are hoping that I send you, and I will not serve you up to them."

While we waited for orders from the King, the General assembled his troops and called for more from the Rhineland. Count Hessi kept to his quarters, which suited me. He quickly returned to his old self, calling for expensive new clothing and complaining the food was not as good as when the King was in residence.

Within the week, the Lippespringe garrison filled with more soldiers, mostly foot soldiers, poor peasants with fields to attend. They could not have been eager for battle.

Word from the King came soon.

"The King has recalled Adalgis, Gallo, and Worad from the campaign against the Sorbs," the General said, tossing the dispatch into the fire. "We are to assemble our force with theirs at the Eresburg fortress to the south. It is a well-fortified Frankish stronghold and a secure place to muster our armies and plan our strategy. From there, we will march up the Weser River Valley for the attack." He gazed into the fire, lost in thought. "At least the devils are not drawing us into the Teutoburg Forest."

Reasons to Fight

Within the week, enough soldiers and supplies for a campaign of several weeks had assembled at the Lippespringe garrison. We set out for the Eresburg fortress. General Theoderic led the march. Hessi and I rode behind him.

"Watch him," the General had told me before we left Lippespringe.

Eresburg was a day's march to the south with a large infantry and supply train in tow. The supply train slowed our progress, but it ensured we would be well stocked with food and necessities and would not have to forage. The timber fortress stood atop the highest hill in the area—more of a mountain than a hill. It had a view over an inaccessible cliff and the Diemel River Valley below. The access point was a steep road that wound up the other side of the hill.

As we rode, the road grew steep and rocky, and the horses strained to carry their riders in some places. General Theoderic signaled a stop and called for one of his captains.

"Use the last company of the infantry to help push the sup-ply carts," he said. "I will lead the rest of the army ahead."

"Yes, General Theoderic," the captain said and spurred his horse toward the supply train.

The road soon leveled, passing through sloping fields teem-ing with soldiers, tents, supply trains, and camp followers. We navigated through a maze of haphazard shelters fluttering and teetering in the breeze. Pallets were laid under wagons and trees for meager protection from the elements. Women tended smol-dering cooking fires and large washing cauldrons. Some hiked their tunics so they could work with less hindrance. Others did it to flash their legs at the soldiers.

Traders crowded the hillside. They were hawking every-thing from shoes to shields and other items made of iron. Weapons, armor, buckles, horse bits, and spurs were in high demand. Wagons were loaded with barrels, tapped to sell beer. Soldiers waited in long lines for beer and clustered around dice games, clinging to women who pushed their breasts close.

We passed though the camp of Worad, Count of the Palace, and his force of Scola horsemen. Adalgis's and Gallo's armies were camped closest to the Eresburg gate, their tents sprawling across the area. The commanders' banners waved above it all, a bear and shield for Adalgis, and a stallion with crossed swords for Gallo.

Gallo's new Scola riders had staked their tents near his own. The youngest boys who had not been promoted to horsemen hauled water, groomed the horses, and cleaned mail armor. I spotted Heric carrying a mail coat up the slope. He placed it in a barrel half full of sand and rolled it down the slope to clean it. The barrel was bigger than he was, and I thought it would get away from him on the hill. He grappled with it to maintain control. The barrel came to a stop at the bottom, and he removed the armor inside. He grunted as he lifted it high enough so it would not drag in the dirt. He carried it into one of the Scolas' tents and returned to roll the barrel up the slope.

Wiping the sweat from his forehead, he spotted me and waved. His face shone with excitement, his anticipation of battle tangible. He, like the other shield bearers, hoped for an opportunity to fight. They would be stationed behind the fighting line, but if things did not go well, they would have to face the enemy themselves. They did not understand what they were hoping for.

On the other side of their camp, I glimpsed Ansgar, wearing freshly cleaned mail. The sun glared off the steel rings, nearly blinding me for a moment. I noticed how it hung loosely from his thin shoulders, accentuating his inexperience. He did not move like a seasoned veteran of combat. He was enthralled with the excitement, making himself vulnerable and an easy target.

General Theoderic was surveying the forces, noting every detail of the muster with a subtle deepening of his creased brow. He was not pleased with what he saw, and I could see why.

"Too many boys and not enough soldiers," I said.

He grunted in agreement. "And where is the Saxon infantry Gallo is supposed to command?" he grumbled. "They likely deserted to join the rebellion too." He reined his horse around to the captain of his guard. "Have my army make camp here."

"But, my lord, there is little room left. We will have to crowd the armies of Gallo and Adalgis."

"Yes, we will," he said.

The General, Hessi, and I crossed a timber bridge into the Eresburg fortress. It spanned a ditch deeper than the height of two men. The fortress wall of earth and rock stood as high as the ditch was deep and was topped by a palisade of sharpened timbers. The gate opened at our approach, and we were greeted by the commander of Eresburg, Count Berinhard.

The General dismounted and the count embraced him with a hearty clap on the back. "Welcome, brother!"

Brother? The General had not mentioned him. The count had an open, friendly bearing and gave his smile freely. He bore little resemblance to his brother.

Berinhard glanced suspiciously at Hessi and turned his attention to me. He grinned. "And is this the Royal Scout of whom I have heard so much?"

The General harrumphed. "This is Tracker, Royal Scout and Huntsman," he said. "He remained at Paderborn this summer to scout and advise me while we complete the Hellweg."

"My lord," I said, lowering my head to the count.

"An honor to meet the valiant saver of the Holy Spear!" He returned my bow, but he was not mocking me. He chuckled with delight. "Even my dour brother speaks highly of you—in his most simple manner." He threw the General a mocking grin. "I hear the Wulfhednar captured you, nearly killed you, and you escaped. Impressive. My scouts do not go far in the Teutoburg Forest. Too many have been found hacked to pieces. There are no good men who are willing to scout for me any longer." The count slapped me on the back. "Someday, I will steal you from my brother. And such wonderful stories you must have! You will have to tell them all tonight at dinner. We are in serious need of entertainment in this godforsaken outpost here. I was sorry to miss the feast the King gave in your honor. Ailing from a bout of the flux, shitting myself until my ass bled like a spiked hog. But I wander a trackless path." He laughed heartily, and the General rolled his eyes.

I think I smiled. His warm manner and levity were welcome after spending so much time in the company of General Theoderic.

"We have more pressing preparations to discuss," said the General.

"Yes, yes, I suppose we must," said the count. "Let us retire to the hall where we can hold counsel. I have sent for Chamberlain Adalgis, Horse Master Gallo, and Count Worad."

The guard escorted us toward the great hall. We passed stables, a smithy, a bake house, storehouses, and housing for soldiers and other residents. On the edge of the cliff stood a watchtower, which had a commanding view of the river valley for many miles. The strategic importance of this fortress was clear; no army could advance on it without being seen.

Next to the watchtower was a simple wooden building. I would have thought it was another storehouse but for the cross on the roof. The simple wooden cross tilted slightly, as if erected hastily, and the roof needed fresh thatching. The door stood ajar, and it was dark inside. A chill breeze blew from inside the place.

Like ice on my neck
Like death on my shoulder

A sacred Saxon temple had stood here, and King Karl had destroyed and buried it under a church. He thought the temple had been the sacred Irminsul—the center of pagan magic. He thought he had devastated it and its power. Only I knew about the far more powerful Irminsul—the giant stone pillar twenty times the height of a men. It had stood with the other Raven's Stones since the beginning of time and could never be buried under a wooden church.

I turned away and followed the others into the great hall. Several shield bearers hustled to help us out of our mail armor. Servants brought food and beer. Brother Pyttel arrived as they poured the beer.

"Brother Pyttel. Welcome!" said Count Berinhard. "Your timing is excellent. I find most monks terribly dull, but you are not like most monks, are you?" He winked, and Pyttel shifted nervously. "I heard that you were sent on another mission into the heathen territory. You must have stories to tell, as does Tracker."

"The Royal Scout and Brother Pyttel are not here to entertain you," said the General. "The monk will bless the commanders' meeting and both will provide counsel."

"Good. We need all the blessings and counseling we can get," said Berinhard, talking with mouthfuls of bread and cheese.

The General scowled at his brother and ordered Hessi to wait outside. The Saxon count obeyed, taking a cup of beer and large piece of cheese.

Berinhard swallowed a large swig and belched. "There are rumors among the soldiers that the uprising is large and well organized. If the rebels take control in the north, you can wager they will soon come south and try to capture Eresburg. Some days, I wish they would."

"This is nothing to jest about," said Theoderic.

The count's jovial expression soured, like a sudden storm moving in. "I am as serious as a cold corpse, brother. These heathens will always loath us for capturing this fortress from them and destroying their sacred temple, the Irminsul. You may be getting long in the tooth, brother, but you have not forgotten how they revolted and retook the Eresburg a year later. It took two years of my life to recapture it and rebuild the fort. It was accomplished under my leadership, using my soldiers—not yours—and I have been stuck here on this rock ever since. It is mine, and I have done what it takes to control it, but I could lose it if this latest uprising is not crushed quickly."

"They will never get this far south," said Theoderic.

Berinhard snorted. "Of course not. Because the King's most favored General is leading the attack." His voice was tinged with sarcasm. "What can you tell us about the leader, Widukind?"

"He has inspired some of the loyal Saxon nobles to turn traitor," he said. "They risk losing much, noble titles and lands granted by the King."

The meeting was interrupted by the entrance of Adalgis, Gallo, and Worad. The shield bearers removed their armor, but the General did not exchange pleasantries and wait for them to be settled with food and drink.

"It appears we have as many generals as soldiers," he said drily. "Horse Master Gallo, where are the Saxon archers under your command?"

Gallo was rubbing his shoulder, freed from the weight of armor. He ignored the General's question, and threw me a scathing scowl. "I will not discuss these matters in front of *him*," he said. "He is lowborn and has no business in this meeting."

I checked my temper, but deepened my voice. "I am the *Royal* Scout and Huntsman," I said. "Answer the question your General asked you."

Gallo waited for the General to refute me, but he did not. Berinhard chuckled and drank deeply of his cup of beer.

Gallo turned his back and spoke lowly to the General, but I heard every word. "Most of my Saxon infantry deserted when they heard about the uprising of their barbaric kinsmen," he whispered. "The best of them left immediately, and the rest fol-lowed quickly."

"You should have sent a detail after them," said Theoderic.

"We did not have the time or resources to track them in unfamiliar woodlands and report here for this muster on schedule." Gallo raised his voice. "Good riddance, I say! They are a traitorous and useless lot of dullards, more trouble than they are worth."

"No man—or woman—who can hold a weapon is entirely useless," said Theoderic. "Your inability to lead has made the Saxons who may have stayed loyal to the King into dangerous enemies. They can provide Widukind valuable information about our movements and numbers."

Gallo buried his nose in his cup of beer. "The King is a buffoon if he thought any of those goat fuckers was ever loyal to him," he grumbled.

Adalgis shook a bony finger. "I warned the King, but he did not take my counsel. I told him those barbarians were not as well in hand as he believed, but he refused to see it. Now we must invade their impoverished lands again to quell them, risking our necks and our soldiers when there is no booty left to collect."

"I have had enough of this," said Gallo. "I will unleash my best armored riders in full force across their lands and trample every one of them into the dirt. We should have done it years ago."

"That is exactly what they want you to do," I said. Everyone gaped at me, but I continued. "If you rampage through their homesteads, you will see how quickly the Wulfhednar will draw you into a fatal ambush in the thickets and swamps."

"I would listen to him," said Berinhard. "Tracker knows the heathens far better than any of us."

General Theoderic ignored his brother. "The Wulfhednar have grown bold enough to massacre a dozen of my Scola riders on the open road in broad daylight," he said.

"Imagine the games the devils will play with any commander who thinks he can take them in their own forest with only one contingent," said Berinhard.

The General unrolled a large map. "The best way to combat their ambushes is to march into Saxony in full force and take their most significant military target. Widukind has established a fortified rebel stronghold on the top of a mountain in the Süntel Hills." He squinted, leaned back, and pointed to the spot. "The King has commanded us to destroy their fortress and kill the rebel fighters. We are to capture Widukind, if possible. Any Saxons who have stayed in their villages and are not actively fighting will be presumed loyal and spared, for now."

"Foolhardiness!" said Adalgis. "We cannot spare the life of a single suckling babe who will grow up to avenge his people."

"It may come to that," the General said. "If it does, I will give the order, and the decision and the consequences will be on my shoulders. For now, the objective is to crush the rebels. When Widukind is captured or killed and his forces defeated, the rest of the Saxons will fall in line."

Adalgis, Gallo, and Worad exchanged looks of disbelief. They clearly disagreed with him and wanted their armies to raze everything in the path of their invasion.

The General called Count Hessi into the room. The commanders eyed him with suspicion.

"Count Hessi, tell us about the rebel fortress," the General said.

As if he had memorized a speech, Hessi described the rebel fortress on the Hohenstein Plateau exactly as he had before.

Adalgis had not taken his eyes off him since he began talking. "How do we know this Saxon lout is not feeding us a pack of lies?" he asked.

Hessi's hand instinctively flew to his sword belt, but it was empty. The General had not allowed him to carry a sword or even a dagger. His arm dropped awkwardly to his side. "I have proven myself a faithful Christian and loyal subject of the King for many years," he said.

"Other loyal Saxon nobles have joined the rebellion," Adalgis said. "I do not trust him."

Gallo snorted. "He is a boot-licking mongrel who wants more table scraps from the King's table."

The General raised a hand to quiet them. "I will be sending scouts ahead of the army to confirm Hessi's report and to continue tracking the rebels' movements."

"You will see I have proven myself loyal," said Hessi. "I have nothing to hide, so go ahead. Send out your bastard scout dog to sniff around."

Hessi's words struck me hard.

The wolf howls inside
Aching to break free

Heart pounding, blood surging
Rising from deep within the chest
A growl
Snarling
Fangs bared
Rage and fury beyond bearing
Rip him to pieces
Rip them all to pieces

Feed the wolf
Feed the Raven

Gallo jumped and drew his sword, and Adalgis and Worad followed suit.

"So now you set your rabid beast upon your own officers, General Theoderic," said Gallo.

I had jumped too, my hand on my hilt. Every hair on my body tingled with the desire to pull my blade, but I forced myself to leave the sword in its sheath; once I drew steel, I would not be able to stop the Wulfhedinn's rage. It would tear Gallo and all the others to shreds.

Waiting for the General's response, I locked eyes with Gallo. Hessi and Berinhard froze in their seats, watching what would happen next.

"Nonsense," the General said. "Sheath your blades and sit. You are behaving like witless lunatics."

"I always knew he was a filthy animal!" said Gallo. "Now the wolf demon has revealed his real face. He could not hide it forever. Yes, everyone has heard the rumors about this fiend, this Wulfhedinn."

My fingers tightened on the sword hilt, aching to draw it. The Raven's call continued to ring in my ears, bidding me to respond in anger, without thought.

Draw the blade
Attack
Kill him

Feed the Wolf
Feed the Raven

A drop of sweat rolled down my forehead. I balanced on my toes on a cliff's edge. A strong wind pushed me to jump, but I had to resist the urge to throw myself into the abyss where the Raven flew. It took all my strength to keep my balance on the cliff and not drive my sword into Gallo's face.

"You are allowing rumor and fear to trick your mind," the General said calmly.

"I know what I saw!" said Gallo. "His eyes—they flashed red, like the Devil! I saw it."

"I saw fangs dripping with blood," said Adalgis. "As plain as a horse's ass."

Worad had turned white, and I feared Hessi would now confirm their suspicions. His timing would be perfect; he could recover a great deal of favor by telling them my father was Widukind and that I had been initiated into his Wulfhednar pack—if he knew.

Pyttel had been shaking his head, watching silently. "Such superstitious idiocy," he said, rising and coming to my side. He lifted my lips, as if checking the teeth of a horse. I pulled away. "You see?" He cackled, patting my cheek. "No fangs, just the same twisted teeth he has always had." He pulled the cross out from under my tunic. "And no demon could wear the Holy Cross of God. It would burn him into ashes."

"Prove it," said Gallo. "Show us that the Lord's cross is not burning you."

I hesitated, but the General waved his hand, urging me to comply. "Show them, and let us be done with this."

I seethed, pulling off the quilted tunic. Why should I hide it any longer? It was time to let them all see what I had suffered in the name of God and the King.

Adalgis gasped at the sight of the belly gash but quickly collected himself. "I have never seen such a wound," he said.

"It is the axe cut of a Wulfhedinn," I said, glaring at each of the commanders.

"It bears evidence to Tracker's tremendous faith in God," said Pyttel. "He would not have survived such an injury and returned to us without the Lord's blessing."

Gallo grunted, and Adalgis and Worad were silenced. No one denied it as I redressed.

"So, Royal Scout and Huntsman," Adalgis said with a tinge of sarcasm, "share with us all your wondrous wisdom of the way of the heathen barbarians."

"*I* will tell you what you need to know," said the General, "if I deem it necessary."

"As you see fit, my General, cousin to our mighty King Karl," Adalgis said, curling his upper lip. "If you trust this man beast enough to take him to your bosom and make him your scout, so be it. And how many silver pieces from the King's treasury will Count Hessi be expecting this time for his loyalty and information?"

The General pounded the table once with his fist, rattling the beer cups. "Enough!" he said. "I will not ignore reports because you have a distaste for the reporter. We must use all the assets we have to defeat Widukind unless you want these Saxon campaigns to continue for another ten years—and no one's coffers can afford that."

It was a sobering strike.

Pyttel broke in. "We must stop making enemies of one other. There are enough enemies outside this fortress."

"Agreed," said General Theoderic. He called for the guard to escort Hessi out. Then he bent over the map, squinting. "My initial plans for this assault must be reconsidered because we do not have the infantry support I expected from Commander Gallo." He frowned at Gallo and reexamined the map. I could almost see the wheels of his mind turning as he considered strategies. Finally, he said, "We will attack from two directions at the same time, a pincer maneuver."

"We have used this tactic successfully many times," mused Adalgis.

"Yes," said the General, "but we must always assume the Saxons will be watching our movements and that they will try to outmaneuver us. "

"Of course, General," said Adalgis.

The General glared at him. "The Scola horsemen will take the main route and attack the Saxons' camped outside the fortification. The infantry will transport the siege equipment up the gully. Their advance will also cut off Widukind's escape route."

Gallo stood, swaying impatiently back and forth on his bowed legs. "I *will* maintain command of all of my Scola warriors."

"I am keeping the men I have brought too," added Adalgis.

Worad nodded in agreement. General Theoderic had few Scola riders in his army, but no one wanted to weaken his own force by providing him with riders.

Theoderic crossed his arms. "So be it," he said. "Adalgis, Gallo, and Worad will command the primary Scola attack, each keeping their own riders but joining together as a single army. I will lead my personal guard and the bulk of the infantry, including the bowmen and those manning the siege equipment. Berinhard, you will remain here with your force to hold Eresburg."

"What about Hessi?" asked Adalgis. "I trust you will keep him under guard."

"Hessi is not your concern," the General said. "Your priority is to ensure your troops obey their orders. We are advancing through unfamiliar terrain. It is heavily wooded and a prime location for the rebels to lie in wait. Our attack must be coordinated precisely so the armies can reinforce each other in the case of ambush. Deviation from the plan will leave us vulnerable to the rebels' barbaric tactics."

The commanders concurred vaguely. The General's face darkened.

"I will also not tolerate drunkenness and riotous looting and pillaging," he said, "not until after we take their stronghold."

"As if there is anything left to plunder in those Godforsaken lands," muttered Adalgis as the council adjourned.

Advance from Eresburg

The next morning, I accompanied Theoderic to survey the mustered forces.

The Scola riders were well armed with spears, swords, helmets, mail hauberks, and shields. Adalgis led the most experienced horsemen, but Gallo's Scola contingent had more riders. Gallo commanded the newly promoted shield bearers, who had little experience, but he also had a few of the kingdom's best champions. Commander Worad's riders were neither highly seasoned nor inexperienced, falling somewhere in the middle.

The General's army included two dozen Scola soldiers who made up his personal guard. He commanded a few seasoned infantry captains to help lead his levy of foot soldiers. Some of them had horses, but they were not trained for mounted combat, and the captains would have to dismount for battle.

Most of the infantry consisted of free farmers who had been summoned to duty. They carried bows and had daggers, seaxes, or kitchen knives in their belts. Few wore any type of armor, and if they did, it was old and worn. Most of the men had a shield, often homemade and without insignias or decoration. None had swords. Some did not have shoes.

"No matter," the General said, but his face darkened, and the rolls on the back of his neck deepened.

The infantrymen bowed as we passed. I overhead one of the captains say, "We are fortunate. General Theoderic can accomplish more with old men with wooden pitchforks than that horsefucker Gallo can do with a whole army of riders."

I grinned, sure the General had heard it too. He tipped his head toward the infantrymen and reined his mount to the archers' practice field. The archers were shooting at man-shaped targets made of straw. They drew their bows with robust forearms and placed hearty bets on their accuracy. They chided one another for less-than-perfect shots, although most of them hit the straw men in the heart or head.

A smile dangled on the corner of General Theoderic's lips. "They may not have horses or swords, but years of hunting for small game have honed their shooting skills."

"Widukind's army consists mainly of lower-class freemen—also masters of the bow," I said. "Adalgis is overconfident his army of horsemen can crush the rebel bowmen."

At that moment, an arrow hit the face of a target, splitting another arrow down the middle.

"Yes, he is," Theoderic said. "That is why I need to you to perform a specific duty. After our forces divide to begin the assault, I want you to trail Adalgis."

"You are not sending me to spy on the rebel stronghold?"

"No, the King has sent his scouts to verify what Hessi has told us. I do not want you to get too close to the rebels." His gaze caught mine. "You are too valuable to me to lose."

I smiled, but he did not return it.

"Watch Gallo's and Worad's movements too," he said. "Report back to me immediately if any one of them deviates from the plan."

"You distrust them?"

"You do," he said.

"There are few I trust in this world."

"A wise choice," he said. "But there are other factors at play. The commanders respect me because they must, but they have no love for me. They are also arrogant and brash because King Karl is master of the Holy Spear. The relic makes them all prone to let impudence lead their decisions. If they do, I do not want to be surprised."

The next morning, King Karl's scouts thundered into Eresburg, bringing news of the rebels' preparations. The General sat in the hall behind his table of maps, cracking his knuckles as he listened to their report. Everything was exactly as Count Hessi had reported, including the number of amassed rebels and the features of Hohenstein Plateau and the surrounding terrain.

"They are preparing for both open battle and defending a siege," one of the scouts said. "We have seen no signs indicating they are planning an ambush."

The vein in the General's forehead pulsated. He was unconvinced—not because he doubted the King's scouts, but because he distrusted Hessi. I knew he would never allow himself to become gullible to the Saxon lord.

"Barbarians are *always* planning an ambush," he said to me after they had left.

He gave the order for the army to advance the next morning. As dawn was breaking, Pyttel and his priests walked by the ranks of soldiers, blessing them and their weapons. Pyttel blessed my sword, and the General allowed him to bless his, but his focus was not on the prayers. He set his sharp jaw and stewed about earthly concerns. He must have been considering how to overcome the loss of Gallo's Saxon infantry and the dissent among his commanders.

I began the journey with him at the head of the combined army, fully armed and riding a new mount. I wished I could be riding Blitz. I pictured her running free in sunny meadows of tall grass far away from here and smiled.

We took the road northeast from Eresburg, following Diemel River. It would be a two-day march to the place where the small stream flowed into the Weser River. There, we would follow the Weser north to the Süntel Hills where the Hohenstein Plateau and the rebel stronghold were located.

I rode quietly next to the General, waiting for him to send me on patrol, but he kept me close. Instead, he sent small details to ride ahead for a mile or two at a time and report back. He reminded his commanders often to keep their captains and their companies alert and aware of the threat of ambush.

We both knew the Saxons were watching our movements and could strike at any time.

The first day passed without incident, and we rested well that night. We made good time the next day. By late afternoon, we came to the confluence of the rivers and stopped to make camp. The next morning, we would follow the Weser River north to meet our fate.

Awake

Fingers of moonlight shot through the holes in the tent. I pulled my mantle over my head to block the light. Better, but the moon still would not let me rest. I turned several times and lay there—awake.

The hours passed slowly. I grew hot under the mantle and flung it off, but I could not evade the heat. Finally, I could stand it no longer. I rose and slipped out of camp. I needed to be out in the night air. Let those who could lose themselves in sleep lie peacefully. Let them find my tent empty and my pallet cold in the morning. They would wonder, and they would talk. Let them think I had deserted again.

I scoured the moonlit sky before stealing into the shadows. She was not there, not the black wings nor the screech chilling my spine.

The breeze carried me into the forest, where I had slept for many years before coming to the Frankish King. I floated, as if disconnected from my body. Sweating, I tore off my boots and returned to the ground, and the moss-covered earth cooling my bare feet. I peeled off my clothes like a butterfly shedding its cocoon, but instead of flying, I dropped to my knees like a dog, a beast.

I scraped aside leaves and branches, tossing a rock. Loosening dirt with my hands, I kicked it behind me with my feet. I dug harder and faster, shoving dirt under my fingernails, tearing my skin. I did not stop until I had made a small depression in the ground. Turning several times, I curled into a ball in the cool earth and closed my eyes. I drifted—finding a dream.

Floating over me
Smooth skin glowing
Midnight hair
Moonlight, silvery radiance
Dancing off curves of breast and hip

Sweet musk and hawthorn

My mind wanted to fight her, but my body needed her, ached for her. I waited deliciously between sweet expectation and the desire to draw her close, her soft skin pressing against mine.

Devouring me in her sweet, musky scent
I draw her near
I drink the taste of her
Sweet musk and hawthorn

Glossy black hair
Black feathers spread behind creamy shoulders
Wings spreading wide
Enveloping me
Blood dripping from her beak
She feasts on the flesh of the dead
Suckling me
As I nourish her
Eyes rolling back into ghoulish gray membranes
Burn scarlet red

She shrieks
Feed the wolf
Feed the raven

Between God and the Devil

Jawoke in the hole, unsure where reality had ended and the dream had begun. Had the witch ensnared me with magic, or had I simply wandered from the camp in dazed sleeplessness? For a moment, I savored the dream of the woman. I licked my lips, tasting the memory, wishing it had lasted longer before the Eater of Souls appeared. It all faded quickly, as all dreams did.

I rubbed my eyes, squeezing the dirt and fogginess out of them. I was filthy, smeared with dirt, leaves falling from my hair. Grabbing my boots and clothes, I dressed and returned to camp. The General was awake and gave me a sideways glance but did not ask questions. I broke down our tent, keeping my hands and mind occupied with the task.

The army was ready to ride by dawn. The weather remained warm and sunny during the three-day march through the Weser River Valley. The General continued to send other scouts to ride ahead, and they returned with promising news. The river was running high and fast from the recent rains, but it had not overflowed its banks. Most of the two-track road was dry, and the small patches of mud would not slow the horses or bog down the wagons.

I was concerned that the river would be too high and the current too swift to cross at the ford. General Theoderic was likely pondering the same question. By the third day, the scouts had made it to the ford and back and said the river was crossable. They also had seen no sign of the rebels. I had remained vigilant during the march and had not sensed the presence of the Wulfhednar or the Raven.

"Perfect conditions for a campaign," I said to the General. I almost added, *too perfect* and *too quiet*.

As we arrived safely at the river ford, the General said, "It seems God is with us."

He did not sound convinced, and I was surprised he had said it. He never referred to divine power when discussing military campaigns; he rarely talked of God at all.

Brother Pyttel reined his horse beside us. "I am glad to hear it, General," he said. "God has not spoken to me for a long while."

The monk *had* behaved quite normally in the past weeks—which was abnormal for him. His episodes of madness could be irritating, but his rantings from his talks with God often hailed events that came to pass. I almost hoped he would begin to babble again. I wanted God to tell him *something*, but the monk remained rational and lucid as we made camp.

After camp was made, the General held another counsel with the commanders to finalize plans for the attack. This time, I was not invited. They left me alone outside his tent, but I refused to eavesdrop. If they did not want me, I did not want to hear what they had to say. Instead, I busied myself by cleaning and oiling my sword.

Pyttel was nearby with a line of solders waiting for him to hear their confessions. Their faces were tense with worry; they were desperate to clear their souls before the assault the next day. No one was assured survival in a campaign, even a winning one. The line was long, and the monk was administering penances quickly, sometimes interrupting their lengthy confessions to do so. He regarded me and the long line and sighed. He told the soldiers he needed to relieve himself, and came to talk to me.

"If you rub your sword any harder, you may wipe off the steel," he joked.

"If you do not give your sinners harsher penances, you will never be rid of them," I retorted.

He laughed. "Do not snarl at me because you were not invited to the commanders' meeting."

"I do not care."

The monk scratched his rounded belly. "Stop sulking. The General is avoiding another confrontation between you and his commanders. He is like a father who must separate his rivalrous children so they do not kill one another."

I sheathed my sword. "I am not a child."

"No, not a child," he said and returned to his line of sinners.

The meeting lasted into the night. Several times there were outbursts of shouting coming from the tent. I tried to close my ears, pretending I did not want any part of it. By midnight, the shouting stopped, and the commanders stormed outside. They did not notice me dozing under a tree in the dark as they passed.

"He may be the King's cousin," said Gallo, "but he is not my master."

"He will make enemies of us yet," said Worad.

Adalgis grumbled, "And he will regret it."

I hated Gallo and disliked Adalgis and Worad, but I did not tell the General what they had said. He knew what his commanders thought of him.

The General told me it had been decided that pincer strategy would go forth as planned. The army would split in half and attack from two directions. The Scola force under the command of Chamberlain Adalgis would cross the Weser River and attack the rebel fortress on the Hohenstein Plateau from the southeast. General Theoderic's infantry would follow the Weser River north and attack from the west.

The General's lips remained tight about anything else discussed at the meeting. My pride kept me from asking about it, and I pretended not to care, but I could see his unease in the blue vein pulsing in his temple.

The next morning, Adalgis's force, which included Gallo's and Worad's contingents, forded the river. They crossed at a place where the water spread wide, and the current nearly stopped. The water rose no higher than the horses' thighs. They waded through it without difficulty to an island in the middle of the stream. They traversed the narrow island and splashed quickly through the ankle-deep water to the opposite bank.

The wagons and foot soldiers crossed more slowly but without incident. Then the entire army advanced forward. After the last man, wagon, and rider had moved out of sight, Theoderic turned to me and said, "Wait until dark and follow them."

"Yes, General." I said, scratching my beard. It had grown in since we had begun the march. The coarse hair was thick and itched fiercely, as it did when it first emerged after shaving. Within a few more days, it would engulf the Frankish-style moustache, thwarting my attempts to maintain the refined grooming of a General's son.

I thought of how Pyttel had compared the General to a father who must manage his quarrelsome sons. Now the father was ordering his favored son to spy on his other children. The task did not settle well with me, and I could not shake a sense of foreboding, as I asked Brother Pyttel to pray for my mission.

I knelt in front of him, and he blessed my sword and me. He pulled the wolf hood over my head, and without hesitation, he consecrated it too. When he had finished, he said, "I will also beseech God to guide Chamberlain Adalgis and the commanders to stay on the path of righteousness."

I stood and crossed myself. "You would have better luck by sacrificing to the gods."

Pyttel frowned at my attempt at a joke. "The pagan gods would never favor these Christian commanders," he said. "Adalgis, Gallo, and Worad walk a sword's edge between God and the Devil, and I daresay Wodan and the gods hope they fall to the Devil's side."

The mad monk was making sense. "Enough of your babble," I said, making the sign of the cross a second time.

I gave him a quick smile and slipped out of camp. I was wearing breeches, my wolf skin, a dagger, and a sword. I needed little else. Armor would weigh me down, and I could steal through the forest better on foot than on horseback. I waded across the river ford to the island, crossed it and the rest of the stream, and slipped into the woods.

It was not difficult to track Adalgis's large army of horsemen, and I followed them to the east until they stopped to make camp. I remained in the fringe of the thick forest of ancient beech trees. It was perfect cover for an ambush. The dense woods could block and confound the senses of the most seasoned guide. The twisted branches stretched out like grotesque arms that could entangle and strangle the unwary. Thick beds of green moss covered the ground in the shadows. Soft underfoot, it muffled the most lumbering steps.

Saxon scouts were likely in the area, watching the army's movements. To avoid encounters with them and Frankish sentries, I did not stray too far into the forest or venture too close to camp. I stayed alert, keeping one eye on the sky for the Raven. Several times, I was sure I heard or smelled something near me—a doe in the brush, a squirrel, the falling of a leaf. My gaze moved constantly, from sky to shadows, scanning everything, vigilant.

Crawling on my belly, I observed the camp from different points. Nothing seemed amiss. Fires were lit, and the malty smell of barley porridge filled the air. Horsemen and their shield bearers raised tents, groomed horses, and sharpened weapons. A dozen horsemen rode into camp from the forest carrying a stag. A few more were dispatched to scout the Saxon camp. Like trained dogs, Gallo and Worad followed Adalgis as he oversaw the operation. So far, they were preparing as planned, getting ready to strike once they received the word from General Theoderic.

I watched through the night, but the camp remained quiet—until the scouts returned the next morning. They charged into camp, calling for Commander Adalgis. He rushed from his tent, buckling his sword belt. They spoke in low tones. I pushed my ears forward, straining to hear their conversation, but I was too far away. Gallo and Worad quickly joined the unplanned meeting, and the discussion grew animated. Clearly, something had changed markedly. I hesitated to move within earshot, not willing to risk discovery.

The commanders soon appeared to come to an agreement. They summoned their captains and ordered them to prepare for attack.

It was too soon. The General's infantry army could not possibly be ready yet. As the General had feared, his commanders were not following his plan.

The nithing horse flashes
Gallops across the air
Neighing, shrieking
Hollow, empty eye sockets
A ghoul
Damns the Christian solders to Hell
A portent of death

A signal horn blew from the camp, and the nithing horse vanished. The horn blew again, louder this time, ordering attack. Word spread rapidly, and the camp became a tangle of noise and activity. Horsemen hastily donned armor and grabbed weapons. They flew onto their horses and joined ranks under the banners of Adalgis, Worad, or Gallo.

They were all going to die.

My first impulse was to find Adalgis and talk him out of the assault, but it would do no good. He hated me and would not listen, and the reasons he had for defying the General ran too deep. I could not deter him—but I might stop the young Scola horsemen and shield bearers from joining the attack.

I crept around camp toward Gallo's contingent, looking for the young Scolas. Someone was trying to shout over the din. His voice cracked with excitement—Ansgar. I moved closer and spotted him across the camp. He was mounted, spinning his horse around, calling jumbled orders to the crowd of young horsemen who had emerged from their tents. Some of them were fumbling to don oversized armor by themselves. Others were being assisted by shield bearers who were not much younger than they were. Against General Theoderic's advice, Gallo had kept all the youths together in a band instead of assigning them throughout more experienced companies.

Ansgar's voice cracked as he struggled to be heard. His young riders whooped and shouted as they scrambled to prepare, forgetting the discipline and routine they had learned. I decided to break cover; no one would care at this point. Dodging the scrambling riders, I dropped the wolf hood and approached Ansgar.

"Tracker!" he exclaimed over the din. "I thought you were with the General and his infantry. Where is your horse and armor?"

I quickly mustered a plausible lie. "I have been sent as a messenger to Adalgis. What is happening here?"

Some of the other young Scola riders recognized me and crowded around. Heric was helping a rider don his armor, but he dropped it and ran to my side.

His cheeks flushed with excitement. "Did you hear? General Adalgis wants the shield bearers to ride in the charge too!"

"What charge?" I asked.

"The scouts say most of Widukind's supporters deserted when they heard of our advance up the Weser River," said Ansgar.

"Deserted? I do not believe it."

"Yes! It is true!" His voice cracked. "There are only a few dozen warriors left protecting the approach to the stronghold, and they are pulling back. Horse Master Gallo says the time to strike is now."

I yanked him off his horse. He felt like a child in my hands. "I know these rebel heathens far better than you do," I said. "They are not deserters. Widukind would not have gathered so many to lose them so quickly. They have been planning this a long time and would not retreat so easily."

Ansgar seethed, twisting out of my grasp. "Let me go, Tracker!" he said. "The commanders say the Saxons are cowards. They are afraid of us, and they are running! We will overrun them easily if we do not wait."

"You do not understand what Widukind and his Wulfhednar are capable of," I said. "They may be baiting Gallo and the other commanders. What if it is a trap? Did you think about that? General Theoderic's infantry is not ready yet to support the Scola riders from the other direction in case of an ambush—and the Saxons are likely aware of it. You cannot do this!"

Ansgar's face fell, as if I had ruined his wedding night. "Horse Master Gallo is my commander, and I will follow his orders," he said, remounting his horse.

"You wanted to kill Gallo a short time ago," I said.

"When I was a child," he said. "Now I am a Scola horseman. I ride as my commander orders."

I wanted to tell them they were all children. I wanted them to see they would remain so until after their first battle—if they survived it—but I relented. I could not stop them now.

"Then you must ride," I said, knowing I might never see many of them again.

He scowled at me and spurred his mount. The others followed in a disorganized line, the shield bearers riding in the rear unprotected by a guard. The noise was nearly overwhelming, hooves galloping, men and boys whooping. I could not see Gallo or Adalgis or their banners through the mass of riders. The camp quickly emptied except for a cloud of dust raised by the horses.

CATHERINE SPADER

I was helpless to stop the boys, and I could not reach the General quickly enough for him to rally reinforcements. The battle would be over before I could backtrack southwest and north to the General's camp. The fastest way to alert him was to ride with Adalgis' charging army. I would have to fight my way through the battle and veer west to the General's camp. If I survived, I might be able to alert the General to attack from the other direction before it was too late. Maybe.

One rider had lagged behind the rest of the army, a small boy struggling to control a large stallion. My heart jumped into my throat. Heric. I rushed to the boy, realizing quickly it was not him but another young shield bearer.

The boy's horse bucked and turned several times, spooked by the rush of other horses and an unsure rider. He grappled with the reins, trying to keep his balance and stay in the saddle. He knocked himself in the head with a shield strapped to his arm, but he held on. The horse neighed and tossed its head, pulling the reins from his grip. The boy's skinny legs clung to the horse, and he managed to stay in the saddle. I grabbed the reins and the bridle, calming the horse.

"Tracker!" he said, grinning until I pulled him off the horse. He fell onto his bottom and made a sour face as I jerked the shield off his arm and threw it to the ground.

"Run back to the Weser River," I said, jumping onto his horse. "Follow the river north until you come to the camp of General Theoderic. Tell him what has happened."

"But I want to fight," he said.

"Do as I say."

His bottom lip quivered, and tears flowed down his cheeks. "But it will take me a long time to find the General's camp."

He was afraid to be left alone, but his chances were better if he did as I said. He would not survive if he joined the battle or sat there and cried.

"I am giving you an important task," I said. "Someone has to warn the General so he can aid in the attack. This is a critical mission. I am entrusting it to you."

The boy managed a smile. "Yes, my lord."

He turned and ran toward the Weser River, glancing back at me. At least one of us might live, I thought. I dug my heels deeply into the horse's ribs. It jumped ahead, anxious to gallop.

The army was farther ahead than I expected. The horse-men were racing as fast as their mounts could carry them. They spurred their horses wildly as if they were pursuing a retreating enemy, but I doubted the rebels had fled.

There was a sudden silence, as if the soldiers, their charg-ing horses, and the whole world had vanished for a moment. A chilling screech filled the stillness.

Like ice on my neck,
Like death on my shoulder

Shadow of black wing
Her beak dripping blood

The wail of a dozen hungry wolves

Feed the wolf
Feed the Raven

I raised my shield, gripping tightly and bracing for the im-pact that was coming. Before I could draw close to the rear of the charge, a hailstorm of arrows pelted the riders. Hundreds flew like a swarm of angry wasps, shot from every direction in the forest. Dozens of men were hit and fell before they realized an ambush was upon them. Many horses were also struck. They tumbled, throwing their riders or crushing them. Other mounts stumbled over the fallen. The screaming of men and neighing of horses filled the air. Panic took hold, and the charge faltered into chaos.

Spears flew into the mass of Frankish riders, and more soldiers fell. Another volley of arrows followed, hundreds more, flying from every direction. Two arrows hit my shield, splitting the wood. The impact nearly knocked me off the saddle, but I gripped my mount tightly with my legs and hung on. I dropped the broken shield, drew my sword, and dodged into the cover of the woods. Blood was dripping off my forearm. One of the arrows had penetrated the shield and cut me. I ignored it and pushed toward the west, trying to circle wide around the attack. The ground sloped downward. If the reports from Hessi and the scouts were accurate, I was getting close to the gully that would lead me to the General's location.

I was alone now in the trees, and the sounds of battle were behind me but still near. I heard more arrows sailing through the air and more shrieks of men and horses when they were hit. The volleys continued for several more waves. A signal horn blared, and a deafening roar erupted from the trees. Men shouted in unison, voices enraged and raw, snarling, snapping, howling. The Wulfhednar.

They called for rebellion and revenge and cried for freedom. Their axes, seaxes, and spears clashed against the blades of the remaining Franks. Soon the clanging faded, replaced by the slashing and chopping of steel against flesh and bone. The sound was far behind me now, but I could still hear the agonizing shouts of the dying.

I was too late. The General could not send reinforcements and mount a counterattack in time, but I spurred ahead.

Ahead of me was a wide break in the trees—the gully. As I came to the edge of it, I saw a rider riding ahead of me toward the General's camp. He clung precariously to his horse, grasping his shoulder. I galloped after him. Drawing close, I saw an arrow in his shoulder and the mail coat of a commander. It was Commander Worad.

His face was pale and his eyes darted with panic. "Tracker," he gasped with a wheezing sound. "Get me to the General."

I took his reins and did not waste time asking him why he was alone without any of his men. I knew that he had abandoned them once he had been hit.

He doubled over, clinging to his saddle. We rode quickly, and I did not care if he fell. As long as we were outside the General's camp, we were in danger—and vulnerable to Saxon arrows and spears. The rebels could be anywhere, although Widukind had likely kept most of them focused on the attack in the hills.

As we neared the camp, the sounds of sawing and hammering filled the air. Theoderic's infantrymen were building siege equipment to prepare for the assault.

I reported immediately to General Theoderic in his tent. Worad lagged, shaky on his feet. The General was studying his maps. He grimaced faintly, anticipating the worst of news.

"Adalgis has launched the attack and was ambushed by the rebels," I said. "The entire army is surrounded and trapped high in the hills."

The General dropped the map. "Worad, what the Devil happened?" he demanded.

Worad raised his gloved hand to the arrow in his shoulder and groaned when he touched it. "Our scouts reported that many of the Saxons were deserting Widukind and that the remaining line had retreated," he said. "Commander Adalgis thought the time was ripe to attack, but we were ambushed." He wobbled on his feet and sat on a stool.

The General made no acknowledgment of his injury. "How many rebels?"

Worad groaned. "Difficult to say. So many stayed under cover. We were pelted with arrows from archers hidden in the trees. They did not reveal themselves and gave us no target to fight."

The General bristled with fury. "How many?"

"Perhaps—thousands."

The General was dumbstruck for a moment. "*Thousands?*"

"Our scouts assured us—"

"Widukind let your scouts see what he *wanted* them to see," the General snapped. "He baited you into a trap."

Worad whimpered. "But Adalgis and Gallo were sure they could overrun the remaining Saxons easily."

The General slapped him across the face, knocking him off the stool. "Did you really think it would be so simple? You have the brains of a common toad. Now I must risk my infantry to support your idiocy. There is no time to prepare an organized attack or mobilize siege equipment to capture the fortress."

Worad held his burning cheek and did not rise off the floor. "We jumped at the chance to capture Widukind and his witch, for you, for the King," he said defensively.

"No, you all jumped at the opportunity to grab the glory of defeating Widukind yourselves."

Worad's lips fell open, unable to find words of defense.

"As I thought," the General said. "Tell me what happened, all of it."

Worad's face had grown paler, and his lips were colorless. Blood soaked his tunic from the arrow wound in his shoulder.

"Adalgis's and Gallo's forces were surrounded and pinned down by countless volleys of spears and arrows," he said hoarsely. "My contingent was charging on the western flank, closest to the gully, and I was able to flee. Some of my men may have retreated behind me, but I am afraid that route was cut off for Adalgis and Gallo." He lowered his head.

Theoderic cracked his knuckles as he listened. When he had popped every one of them, he said, "Pray the arrow in your shoulder poisons your blood and kills you before you have to answer for this."

He stood and called for his shield bearer to bring him his armor and sword. "This does not surprise me," he said as the youth helped him into his mail coat and buckled protective greaves over his boney knees. "Hessi fled last night. Pyttel said it was an ominous sign. The madman was correct, and I was justified in not having faith in my commanders."

For a moment, weariness weighed heavily on the General. The bags under his eyes deepened and the pallor in his face grew worse. Once his armor was on, he stood straight, cleared his throat, and barked orders. "Sound a call to arms. Assemble the captains—and Tracker—you will need your boots and armor." As an afterthought, he added, "Summon the physician for Commander Worad."

The captains were given their orders, and the infantry quickly mustered in file formation to ascend the narrow ravine. Theoderic rode at the front of the army, refusing a safer place in the line. I rode with him, protected by helmet, shield, and countless tiny rings of steel. I carried my sword, a spear, and a dagger.

As we rode up the gully, we saw several Frankish Scola horsemen galloping downhill. They had been struck with arrows to the arms and legs but rode sturdily into the protection of our force.

"More are coming," one of them said. "Some have lost their horses and are trying to escape on foot."

"Shields!" the General ordered. The trumpeter sounded the horn to raise shields as we advanced.

Several more horsemen galloped down the gully. Moments later, a small volley of arrows flew toward us from the thick forest ahead. They fell short of our advance. The General ordered the archers to cover the retreating Scola riders. They shot blindly into the woods ahead, and it stopped the Saxon volley long enough to allow the riders to reach us safely.

We advanced slowly up the gully to allow the infantry to keep their shields raised. More Scola riders appeared, and the General signaled for another volley to cover their retreat. Despite this, several horses were hit by arrows shot by Saxon archers hidden in the forest. The horses stumbled or reared, throwing their riders. A few men scrambled to their feet and ran or limped toward the safety of the infantry line. More stragglers ran on foot, having lost their horses. Many were hit and fell. They writhed on the ground, struggling to rise or crawl to safety, but they were easy targets for the unrelenting waves of arrows.

"Our own archers have no distinct target," General Theoderic said. "There is no way to organize a shield wall in this narrow chasm. The best we can do is to protect the retreat of the survivors."

He ordered the men to advance a dozen paces. We were now in range of the rebels' arrows. The volleys increased without respite, falling upon us like a cloudburst. Many arrows found their way between the shields and hit our infantry.

"From the number of arrows, it is obvious we are outnumbered," the General said from under his shield. "The devils are too clever to break cover and fight us in open battle. We have no choice but to retreat out of range."

We pulled back as more survivors emerged. They had all been injured and crawled or stumbled toward us. They were all shot with multiple arrows long before reaching the army's protection.

We retreated to the relative safety of our fortified camp. Theoderic dispatched a messenger to the King with word of the ambush. Then he ordered the surviving army to pull back to the security of Eresburg.

Only God Can Forgive Them

*T*he remaining army was garrisoned inside the walls of Eresburg. The air was heavy with the stink of festering wounds, horseshit, and fear. The time was ripe for the rebels to march south and take the Frankish-held stronghold. We reinforced the gate, although it would not keep the rebels out for long if they attacked. There were too many of them. We could do little more than hide behind the walls and pray to God until the King sent reinforcements to our rescue.

No one talked of the fallen men who were rotting in the sun on the Hohenstein Plateau. The General had not ordered a party out to recover the bodies. There were not enough men left to guard such an endeavor against the huge rebel force, and no one believed they would allow us to collect our dead in peace.

General Theoderic had sequestered himself in his quarters and had spoken little since the retreat. He left the training of the remaining forces to his brother Count Berinhard. I rarely saw the General, and when I did, his face was gaunt and drawn. The circles under his eyes had grown dark, and he limped more heavily on his wounded leg. It had not healed properly, but he still refused to let a physician care for him.

King Karl's written response to the massacre came within days. I read his dispatch to General Theoderic and Count Berinhard.

"There must not be a moment's delay in avenging this wickedness by the murderous, treacherous heathens. I am assembling my entire army and will march to join you at Eresburg within several weeks. Until then, you are to hold the Eresburg, train hard, and prepare for a full-force invasion of Saxony."

"He has been shamed, as have we all," the General said.

The King arrived at the head of the largest military force I had ever seen. His army train spread all the way to the bottom of the Eresburg mountain and several miles through the river valley.

He gripped the Holy Spear fiercely in his right hand as the gates were opened for him. His expression was wrathful, and his sapphire blue mantle whipped harshly in the wind. No one was looking forward to greeting him.

He called an immediate meeting with Worad, who was struck with fever from his shoulder wound. It lasted half the night, and in the morning Worad left Eresburg with an armed escort, exiled from court. He was so weak two he had to ride in a wagon. He would not survive long.

After Worad left, the King pressed me for every detail of the campaign, from the muster at Eresburg to the retreat from the Hohenstein Plateau. He paced impatiently as I told him of the ambush and the locations of the fallen. I also told him what

I had learned when spying on Adalgis's army. He listened intently, but did not offer his usual friendly banter. He then held a council to plan the invasion of Saxony. It included the General, the captains he had brought with his army, and me.

The captains offered various strategies for the campaign. Tapping his fingers impatiently on the table, the King did not acknowledge any of their ideas, and the General's face remained like stone. No one proposed attacking the Externsteine, Widukind's lair and the heart of rebel activity. It was the most logical target, but without a completed road, the army could not get to it through the impenetrable Teutoburg Forest. Moreover, everyone was afraid to suggest it. After the disastrous ambush, they feared the Wulfhednar and the dark magic of the forest more than ever. I could see it on their faces as each one tried his best to suggest a viable campaign strategy that did not involve attacking the Raven's Stones.

The King had heard enough. He jumped in a rage, his face flushing, and threw his stool across the room. It splintered against the wall.

"Useless!" he bellowed. "You are all worthless! We must crush Widukind and the Wulfhednar if we are to crush this rebellion. If it requires sending the entire army into the Teutoburg Forest single file, I will do it. If it requires the annihilation of every living Saxon—"

The captain of the Eresburg guard broke into the meeting, leading Count Hessi by a tether around his neck. The count's hands were tied behind him, and his tunic was torn and soiled by a bloodied nose.

"This Saxon pig boy came to the gate, saying he has a message for the King from the rebels," the guard said. "My men would have beaten him to death if I had not stopped them."

"My King," Hessi pleaded, falling to his knees. "I bring good news."

The King ordered the guard to leave.

"The rebel army has disbanded in panic," Hessi said. "They are afraid you will invade with your full army to retaliate. The Saxon nobles and I have convinced many of them to surrender. They are gathering at the Saxon settlement of Verden, north of the Süntel Hills, to welcome their King, lay down their arms, and swear fealty to you. Over four thousand rebels and non-rebels are submitting and will agree to any terms you propose—in exchange for mercy."

"Are Widukind and his Wulfhednar there to submit to me?" the King asked.

"Widukind and his Wulfhednar are in hiding. No one knows where they are."

I did. They were at the Externsteine, protected by the magic of the Walkyrie. I felt it in my heart and in the hole in my gut, but I said nothing.

The King stroked his long golden-red moustache a half dozen time before speaking. "Go back to Verden and tell them this: Widukind and his Wulfhednar will be held accountable," he said. "The rest will be exonerated, and anyone who is useful in bringing in Widukind and the Wulfhednar will be rewarded."

Hessi bowed. "Thank you, my King."

"You will also tell them anyone who shelters or aids Widukind will wish that he never drew breath. I will arrive in Verden with my full army within the week to accept their surrender. Tell them if I see one child draw a kitchen dagger, we will attack and give no quarter to anyone. Are these terms clear, Count Hessi?"

"Yes, my King," he bowed. "I will take my leave and prepare for your arrival at Verden."

The King dismissed him and said, "There will not be another humiliation like we suffered at Süntel. Make no mistake; we will enter Verden weapons drawn, surround the rebels, and hold them until Widukind and his main leaders are handed over."

"Will the rest be pardoned?" I asked.

The King drove his dagger into the table. "Only God can forgive them now."

The Rider

It was decided we would gather the bodies of the fallen on the way to Verden, under the protection of the King's large army.

I was not afraid to return to the site of the ambush, but I dreaded it. We marched slowly to the site, hampered more by reluctance than the heavy wagons brought to collect the bodies. As we crossed the Weser, black clouds were building to the west. The wind turned over, bringing a storm. We were going to get soaked.

Lightning flashed and thunder boomed in the distance. The storm grew in intensity, drawing near and making the company uneasy. Despite the building storm, I stayed watchful for stray rebels who might be lurking in the forest. I saw no sign of them until we neared the ambush site.

At the top of the ridge, a rider appeared bearing a black banner. Lightning flashed, and a bolt stuck the ground nearby. I blinked, and the rider was gone. Had I imagined it?

"Did you see that?" I asked the horseman next to me.

"See what?"

"The rider at the top of the ridge. You were looking directly at it."

"There was no rider," he scoffed.

Thunder struck and an unearthly screech echoed through the air. It was answered by countless shrieks and screams, the voices of the hungry. A flock of black ravens rose like a black cloud from over the ridge. The rider reemerged, closer, clearer this time. It was a woman, her black banner unfurling into the wings of the Walkyrie.

I gripped the arm of the horseman. "There!" I said. "There she is!"

He shook his head. "All I see are ravens, eating the remains of our comrades!" he said, turning his mount and falling to the back of the line.

The Walkyrie spurred her horse over the ridge and was gone.

I smelled the stink long before we saw the first body. The area was covered with the dead, and the stench of rotting corpses made my eyes water. They had been stripped of armor, weapons, and clothing by the Saxons. Much of the flesh had been peeled and pecked by the ravens, and maggots and beetles were slowly devouring the rest. Many had had been taken by arrows, but others were decapitated and mangled from axe, spear, and sword. It would be difficult to identify all of them. It began to pour, the sky emptying tears on us as if the heavens were crying.

I spurred ahead, following the trail of putrid men and rotting horseflesh to a small stream. There I found the remains of Ansgar, little Heric, and the other young horsemen.

The boys' bones and bits of flesh lay scattered around the body of Gallo, where they had made a last stand against their attackers. They had lost their horses and encircled their commander on foot, facing certain death to protect him—a man who had betrayed their trust and had led them into disaster. They had been raised to the level of Scola before they were ready and given their oaths to follow their commander. They had kept their word, dying with honor as men, now fodder for scavengers.

Tears were stinging my eyes. I wiped them with my forearm, and the Raven flew above. The Walkyrie reappeared over the ridge, riding in full armor, like a ghostly soldier. She sat tall in the saddle and raised her sword, as if in salute. The rain washed away my tears and erased her image.

I should have prayed to God for the boys' souls, but I knew the Walkyrie had taken the boys under her care. The Christian youths, though reckless, had fought and died with honor and courage. They were better suited to Wodan's great hall in Walhalla than the Christian God's heaven.

I could not hate the Saxons for this. I despised Gallo, as if he had murdered the boys by his own hand. I wanted him to rot where he lay. He did not deserve a Christian burial—or a place in Walhalla.

An armed contingent took the remains to Eresburg. The death toll included every man and boy under the command of Adalgis and Gallo, and many from Worad's contingent. The body of the small boy I had sent to warn the General was found nearby. Among the fallen were twenty four other high-ranking nobles—most of them comrades or extended family of the King.

The King's Orders

From the massacre site on the Hohenstein Plateau, King Karl headed the march north, deep into the heart of Saxon territory. He was fury embodied, ordering the destruction of every Saxon farm, field, and village we passed. Word had spread quickly, and the local Saxon farmers fled ahead of the invasion. The deaths of the shield bearers and young Scola riders weighed heavily on me. I was weary of death and glad there were no Saxons in our path to fight and kill.

The smoke and char in the air blocked the sun. The odor burned my nose and made me cough, and the stink of it troubled me. Not every farmer in every one of these villages was a rebel, yet they were punished just the same.

We followed the Weser River north to where it flowed into the Aller River. On a hill overlooking the meeting of the rivers was the fortified Saxon town of Verden. A large field lay below the town, and it was crowded with Saxons. They had pitched their tents randomly and had not set a guard around the camp.

The King ordered his army to draw arms but not to attack. The Saxons watched us—and our drawn blades—as we rode through their camp. In a wave of movement, most fell to their knees and bowed their heads to the King, some prostrating themselves. They looked unarmed, and the gate of Verden was open and without guard, indicating surrender.

Hessi greeted us outside the gate. He was accompanied by a dozen of his nobles, without weapons or an armed escort. He held his head high, despite his bruised and swollen nose.

"My King, welcome," he bowed deeply. "As promised, they have come to submit, and my patrols have captured some of the leaders and key instigators, who I will turn over to you. The rest here, camped on the fields, are lesser nobles and freemen, mostly farmers. There are more than four thousand, unarmed and ready to submit to you. It is difficult to tell who among them actually participated in the uprising, but guilty and innocent are formally yielding as a sign of loyalty and—"

The King did not give pause. "Where is Widukind?" he demanded.

Hessi hesitated. "Many of the leaders who incited the rebellion are here—"

"Where is Widukind?" The King repeated.

"My soldiers are scouring Saxony for him," said Hessi

The King jammed his finger at Hessi. "You let him escape!"

The count cowered. "Please, my King. I assure you they will track him quickly. No one would dare offer him protection now."

The King reined his horse toward us. "General Theoderic, round them up—all of them. Begin taking heads. Do not stop until someone reveals where Widukind and his Wulfhednar are and is willing to take us to him."

"Yes, my King," the General replied without pause.

Hessi protested. "But, my King, these people have surrendered and laid down their arms in good faith," he said. "They were promised—"

"Traitors do not deserve promises."

"But not all of them supported the rebellion, and many of those who did so were desperate or pressured by Widukind and the Wulfhednar. I have the instigators of the uprising under arrest within Verden. Take them for punishment."

The King scowled. "They will be punished soon enough. If the rest of these Saxons are truly faithful to God and loyal to me, they will reveal Widukind's location and those who aided him before a single head hits the ground. If they do not, you will watch every one of them die before baring your own neck for the axe."

The King ordered the arrest of Hessi and his nobles. Unarmed, they were quickly subdued.

"I am no rebel," one of the nobles said. "It is Hessi you want. He conspired with Widukind to draw you into the ambush."

"He tried to get us to conspire with him, but we refused," said another noble. "We are innocent! We followed the path of your God and have done everything you have asked of us."

"You did not bring me Widukind or inform me your lord, Count Hessi, was a traitor," the King said. "You have done nothing, which makes you guilty in the eyes of God."

He spurred his horse violently, and his personal guard followed. They galloped across the field to the top of a rise that had a clear view of the area. The General met with me and his captains and laid out the King's plans.

"I thought we came to take the pagans' surrender," one of them said.

"The King has changed his mind," said the General. "He lost many of his best commanders and close friends at the hands of a force of low-born heathens. The act demands blood revenge, for the honor of those who have been lost and for his honor—and ours."

Some of the captains nodded and others smiled. One stepped forward. "Good. I am bloody tired of these traitorous heathen animals. I say, let us be rid of them all."

"The sooner the better," another said, fingering the grip of his sword.

I had listened to their conversation, watching the thousands of unsuspecting Saxons who crowded the field. They were trusting King Karl to keep his word and accept a peaceful surrender. I could keep quiet no longer.

"I too crave vengeance," I said, "for the senseless deaths of the young Scola riders and all the soldiers who were led by treachery. I would wring it from the necks of those responsible—Horse Master Gallo and Chamberlain Adalgis. They brought defeat upon themselves and went against *your* orders, General."

Theoderic spurred his horse roughly. His demeanor demanded I follow him, and a frosty silence fell between us as we rode. We stopped at the edge of the forest, out of earshot of the armies.

"You *will* help carry out the orders of your King, bearer of the Holy Spear, who does the bidding of God," he said.

I looked over the field of Saxons, some of them rebels, some not. I was unsure what I wanted to see. An answer? Was this truly God's will? The Lord had not spoken to me or allowed me to feel His grace. A reply would not come from Him. I had to find my own answer.

The General continued, "You will oversee the beheadings. The first head will fall under your axe, and you will ensure every one of the bastard devils is cleaved at the neck."

"You give this task to me?"

"I have seen no one more skilled at beheading than a Wulfhedinn."

"I am not a Wulfhedinn! I am your son."

"And this will be the final test of your loyalty."

Test of loyalty? I had nearly died returning the Holy Spear to the King, and I had been forgiven my sins. I had cast off the wolf skin, shaved my face, and donned the woven tunic of a Christian nobleman. I had spied, scouted, fought, and killed in the King's name. I had served faithfully and done everything asked of me and more. I had defied death and the demons of Wodan to return to my place among Christians.

"I need no further test of my fidelity," I said.

The General's stone eyes bore into mine. "Are you refuting the orders of the King who bestowed honor upon you, elevated you from a filthy exile to a high position in his court?"

I thrust my chin forward. "Yes."

"Do not dishonor yourself," he said. "It is time you prove who you are: Tracker, the noble Royal Scout and Huntsman and my adopted son, or Gerwulf, the filthy beast." He looked at me as if I were an animal to be used as he saw fit. "Decide quickly," he said.

The Raven soars overhead
The wolf howls

Feed the wolf
Feed the Raven

Anger, hurt, and defiance raced through my body. He had not really accepted me as his son and would never do so, even if I cleaved a thousand Saxons necks. My head pounded, and my heart hammered against my chest. I hungered to lash out at him. I longed to answer the call of the Raven, but this was not the time—not yet.

"I am your son, my lord," I said. Could he hear the lie in my voice?

"Good," he said. "Now go. Ensure the King's orders are carried out."

I rode around the perimeter of the field. The Scola horsemen were encircling the Saxons with spears readied. The infantry followed, creating a solid shield wall behind the riders. The Saxons grew restless when they saw the Frankish force surrounding them, poised for attack.

One of the Scola riders announced to the crowd, "We want the location of the rebel leader Widukind. Anyone who can lead us to him will be rewarded. If no one is willing to hand him over, everyone will suffer the punishment."

Dissension spread quickly through their crowd. Tension filled the air, but no one stepped forward to offer information about Widukind's whereabouts. The Saxons shouted, spat, and cursed the King and the horsemen. Some panicked and drew small blades they had hidden under their mantles. Others ran to their tents and retrieved seaxes they had stashed there.

The Scola riders moved in, tightening the circle around the mass. They whooped and hollered, driving the Saxons like cattle from their campsites and trampling the tents. Some Saxons shouted with outrage that they had submitted in good faith to the King. Others invoked the names of Wodan and Saxnot and other pagan gods, cursing the Franks and King Karl. The noise became deafening as they were boxed in by the Frank-ish army. The Frankish horsemen quickly impaled those who had drawn a weapon or refused to move. As blood flowed, the Saxons panicked.

I scanned countless Saxon faces as they scrambled to avoid the horses' hooves and the riders' spears. Most of them were peasants, not warriors, and not all of them were rebels. Most were frightened, desperate farmers trapped between the wars of greater men.

Some of the Saxons tried to break through the line of Scola riders. They were quickly killed or trampled. A few made it past the horsemen, but the infantry line immediately gutted them with spears and axes. I wanted no part of this massacre, and I could not stop it.

I spotted one of Hessi's patrols riding toward the field, lead-ing a dozen prisoners. Their hands were tied behind them and their necks were bound to a log laying across their shoulders. They were bloody and bruised. One of them was wearing little more than a blood-soaked wolf skin. The patrol had hobbled his legs closely together.

I raced to the patrol, squinting to see the face of the warrior in the wolf skin. Had they captured Widukind? I broke out in a sweat, fearing the answer but needing to know.

His face was smeared dirt and ash to blend his features into those of the wolf hood, to become one with the beast. As I pulled alongside the patrol, I saw he was not Widukind, but he was a Wulfhedinn.

"I am King Karl's Royal Scout and Huntsman," I said. "General Theoderic has put me in charge of the captives. Who are these men?"

"More instigators of the uprising," the captain said. "One of them is a Wulfhedinn," he added, pointing at the man in the wolf skin.

The whites of the Wulfhedinn's wild eyes bulged with rage.

"Bring him to me," I said.

"He is a demon," the soldier warned. "He will kill you."

"He will not. Bring him."

Reluctantly, he agreed.

He and his soldiers bound the Wulfhedinn's hand fetters to the hobbles on his legs before untying him from the log. As soon as he was freed, the soldiers yanked his hobbles, pulling his legs out from under him. He fell, and they quickly kicked him several times and tightened the restraints until he was bound helplessly, wrists to ankles behind his back.

He had deep slashes on his chest and arms and was pale from bleeding. Despite this, he writhed on the ground and spat at me with more spite than a wolf caught in an iron trap.

I ordered the soldiers to leave us. They raised their brows as if I was crazy, but they obeyed. They moved on with the other captives, groaning under the extra weight they now carried.

"You are Wulfhedinn?" I asked the rebel.

He growled. "You know who I am, brother," he said with a raspy voice.

Brother

The witch had said we were brothers and had cut us and mixed our blood. I thought she had poisoned and bewitched me to steal my will and make me one of them. I had believed it ever since that night.

I bent close to him and whispered, "The King is seeking blood vengeance on every Saxon on this field for the massacre on the Hohenstein," I said. "He will behead them all unless someone tells him where Widukind has fled."

He seethed. "These peasants have surrendered and were promised clemency!"

"The King is not interested in farmers," I said. "He wants Widukind and his Wulfhedinn followers. Lead us to him, and the King will show mercy on the peasants—and you."

"And who promises this? *You?*" He spat at me. "The one who has turned his back on his own Saxon blood? A Wulf-hedinn who has forsaken the wolf skin to become the slave of the Christian King and his General? You were chosen by the Walkyrie and honored as the son of Widukind. Now you bring the greatest dishonor upon yourself by conspiring to hunt down your own father, your real father."

A dark shadow flew over the field. She was there.

The Raven
Her shadow covers all
The King's killing field
God's killing field

She circled around me, and my soul felt blacker than it had ever been. I watched the Wulfhedinn writhing on the ground, beaten, hog-tied and helpless. I could no longer be angry with the witch, the Walkyrie—Vala. She had not stolen my will; she had been showing me my path. When I chose not to take it, she had stood aside and let me go.

I could no longer deny it.

I had betrayed them all—my father, my people, the gods, Vala. I saw the pain of my betrayal in my blood brothers' eyes and those of every Saxon on the field. Now, I had pleaded for him to hand over his leader, my own father. I knew of Widukind as a rebel and a Wulfhedinn, but he had embraced me as his true son, as his own blood, for exactly who I was.

"No one will tell you where Widukind is," the Wulfhedinn said. "We would rather die now than submit to your King and become what *you* are."

The Raven shrieks
Ringing in my ears
Slicing my spine
Like red-hot iron
Blood on my hands
I could flee
But not escape

I left him with the patrol, vowing silently to return to free him when I could. I rode madly around the field, a mass of angry and terrified men. The crowd had been compressed into a small area by the Frankish soldiers. The noise they made was deafening. Shrieking and shouting, many were fighting back against the Scola horsemen despite their lack of weapons. They were quickly run down and killed. Many more were trying to break through the wall of shields and spears although they were outnumbered four to one. They too were slayed, and they died calling the name of Wodan, who would favor them over those who died as captives.

At the other end of the field, soldiers were sharpening long axes and preparing for the executions. Theoderic had joined the King and his guard at the top of the hill. They were watching to see whether I had fulfilled my duty. I reined toward them to confront the King and convince him to stop this madness.

I passed Brother Pyttel and the priests who had come to offer prayers for the souls of the executed. He called to me. "I was wrong," he said, his face twisted with grief. "You will not become a legend. This King and his massacre will be all the people remember."

"I never wanted any of this," I said. "Not a single Saxon, even those who have been baptized, will accept a Christian blessing now."

The monk ran his hands through his disheveled tonsure. "I know."

"Go to Wodan's Spring," I said. "Make a sacrifice for them, so they can die as proud pagans." I left him, spurring ahead toward the rise where the King sat.

The Scola horsemen began to throw nets over the crowd. They fell on groups of men, tangling their limbs. The captives struggled to free themselves but entangled themselves further, pulling one another down in panic.

The horsemen threw long ropes with large nooses over the men who had not been trapped by the nets. The nooses quickly fell over the fleeing men. The riders yanked on the ropes, tightening the nooses, and pulled the men off their feet. They backed their horses, dragging them by the chest, abdomen, or neck. More nooses flew, and few were able to dodge them. The ones who did were quickly slashed by swords or stabbed by spears.

Deep in the middle of the melee, something caught my eye—a figure unlike others. It was a woman, and she had evaded the nets and the nooses. She was pushing through the crowd trying to find a break in the soldier's shield wall.

I spurred my horse closer. She wore breeches and torn black leather armor. Her long hair was knotted on her head in the manner of a warrior. It was matted with blood that had dripped over half of her face. The rest was darkened with dirt and ash like a Wulfhedinn. I was sure of who she was—Vala.

She would never have surrendered with the peasants. Had she come to summon demons against the King and his army and been captured?

She did not see me. She was too focused on avoiding the nets and ropes. She sidestepped two falling nooses but a third one fell over her head, dropping to her ankles. A Scola horseman jerked the rope and yanked her off her feet. She fell with a hard thud, and the rider spurred his horse and dragged her. She tried to curl into a ball to protect herself. I saw the terror in her eyes. She was not afraid for herself, but for the child she carried. Although her belly was not yet bulging, every movement she made, every emotion crossing her face told me she was with child.

They talk of a prophecy
A special child born in the spring
A descendant of Wodan
A redeemer who will bring the wrath of the old gods down upon all Christians

I had wanted to believe that she had laid like a bitch with the pack of Wulfhednar. The Saxon counts had said she had chosen the strongest of them to father the demon. They had said the father was likely Widukind.

Now, seeing her lying captive and beaten, I heard her voice. It came to me from the sky where the Raven soared and from within, the place deep inside me where the wolf dwelt. It whispered the words that had flowed from her red lips on Midsummer Eve when she had taken me in her embrace.

"I am Vala, warrior, healer, and the Chooser of the Living and the Slain. I am Walkyrie, and I choose you for life."

The Walkyrie had indeed chosen the strongest of the Wulf-hednar to father her child. But it was not Widukind; it was the son of Widukind. She had chosen me, and she carried my baby.

And now she was defeated and would die—not in the honor of battle, but as a helpless captive of the Christians, the people I had chosen as my own. Vala's blood, and that of my child, would be on my hands.

I drew my sword and spurred my horse toward her. I no longer cared about God's grace. I wanted her. I had to have her. She had embraced the savage beast in me. She had shown me to how to embrace the Raven in her and the wolf in myself, but I had rejected her and my true self. I had damned my soul to a far darker place than God could send it.

"Make way!" I shouted, spurring my horse through the infantry ranks toward her.

The crowd of foot soldiers was thick, and their shield wall was solid. Before I could get through, the Scola stopped dragging her, allowing the rope to slacken a bit. Her expression changed from fear to the fury of a wolf mother defending her young. She moved quickly, coiling the slack around her hand. She gave the rope a hard yank and pulled the unsuspecting Scola off his horse. She loosened the rope around her ankles and stood, turning toward me. Her vacant stare looked straight through me, as if I did not exist.

"Bring that woman to me!" I ordered an infantryman.

"There are no women here," he said impatiently.

"I am the Royal Scout and Huntsman, and General Theoderic has put me in charge of this operation," I said. "You will bring her to me!"

I pointed to the spot where she had stood, but she had vanished. I kicked my horse and pushed through the shield wall, knocking over several startled soldiers. They shouted and cursed me as I reined to the place I had last seen her. I rode back and forth through the chaos, dodging clusters of roped and netted men, but I could not find her. The only way to save her was to convince the King to stop the executions.

He and General Theoderic were watching the operation from the hillside. They were sitting back, resting on their mounts, waiting for me to take charge of *their* massacre.

I turned my horse and pushed back through the shield wall. Several Saxons who were loose tried to follow me. When others saw their escape, they rushed to follow them. The shield wall parted slightly to let me through, but the unarmed Saxons were quickly surrounded. The sounds of the soldiers beating them followed me as I galloped up the hill to the King.

The Blood Court

"**W**hy have the beheadings not begun?" the General asked me with a frosty tone.

"My General, many of these Saxons are baptized Christians who have surrendered in good faith," I said.

The King bristled. "They are traitors who broke every oath they took to me and to God."

"Your own commanders, your *friends*, broke their oaths," I said. "They wanted victory all to themselves, so they disobeyed orders and launched their attack without the General and his army. Their pride and greed led them into the ambush. They killed your Scola warriors as surely as Saxon arrows did."

"Be silent!" he boomed. "You, whom I have dubbed my Royal Scout and Huntsman, will return to the field and carry out my orders. Do not cross me in this, Tracker. God calls for justice, and I demand it in His name!"

His face glowed with red fury, and I saw him for the tyrant he had become. He was holding himself as higher than all others, even God. In his great sapphire mantle, he was more of a monster than those who donned the wolf skin.

"This is a massacre, not justice." I tore off my cross, unbuckled my scabbard, and dropped them at the feet of Theoderic. "I can no longer abide by you or your God. I am the son of a Wulfhedinn, the son of Widukind."

There was a moment of stunned silence.

The King thrust the Holy Spear at me. "I will throw you back into the dark hole in Hell from which you came."

A long snapping, snarling shriek
Teeth bared, seething
Peering through the eyes of the beast
Its heart beating inside me
Pounding harder and harder
Muscles surge
Strength rules
Wulfhedinn

You will never be one of them

Unthinking, wild with fury, I wrenched the Holy Spear from the King and thrust the tip against his throat. "Stop the beheadings!" I snarled. "Give the order!" My voice came from deep inside my chest, harsh and dripping with rage and madness. I had no fear of the King, the General, or the royal guard.

The King's eyes were wild with fear, his face taut with panic. His life was in my hands. One quick stab through his throat, and I would condemn him to die by his own precious relic.

His guards froze. There were terrified I would tear their King's throat out—and their own—if they made a step toward me.

"Take him!" Theoderic ordered.

I pressed the spear harder against the King's throat. "Stop the beheadings!" I demanded.

The King swallowed deeply, his upper lip trembling as if fright had stolen the words from him. He had said he did not fear me, but until now, he had not known how ferocious I could be when I called upon the Wulfhedinn. For a moment, I held supreme power over him, his guard, and the General.

Then something fell over me, tangling my arms and legs— a net. I dropped the spear and thrashed, trying to free myself, but a hard blow struck me from behind and knocked me off my horse. I hit the ground hard, gasping and flailing under the net. The more I struggled to free myself, the more tangled I became. I growled and snapped rabidly to keep the guards at bay, and it worked for a brief time.

"Subdue him, so I can flay him alive," the King ordered.

I was jabbed in the chest by the blunt end of a spear, break-ing my ribs. Someone kicked me in the back and the head. An-other boot battered my face and gut. I curled into a ball to de-fend myself, and the beating continued until I fell into darkness.

I did not know how much time had passed when I awoke. It was dark. I lay on my side, my hands and feet bound behind me. Tied like a hog, I had been stripped of my armor and my clothing.

Blood and dirt congealed on my face. Through gritty eyes, I saw the glow of large bonfires spreading out across the field. The flames crackled and popped, shooting glowing embers into the night sky. The smell of blood hung in the air.

Someone was standing nearby with his back turned. I blinked, trying to clear my sight. The man was holding a sword. I blinked again. It was my sword, the General's gift.

"I gave you everything, even my son's sword," the General said with spite. "You murdered my son and tried to take his place. You betrayed me—like all the rest of them."

I spat blood and dirt from my mouth. Coughing, I cleared my throat and whispered with a gravelly voice, "I was never your son. You used me. You betrayed *me*."

"I leave you to your fate, Wulfhedinn. No god can save you now."

He limped away on the injured leg that had never healed. The wound would have killed the old bastard if not for me. I hoped it pained him with my memory for the rest of his life.

I was left with a lone guard to stand watch over me. My vision slowly cleared, and I could see farther out onto the field. It was quiet except for the crackling of the fires.

Like ice on my neck
Like death on my shoulder

The guard abruptly dropped his spear and threw his head back. Grunting, he wavered on his feet and fell to his knees. Behind him stood a dark figure, a monk's cowl pulled over his head and face.

Brother Pyttel.

He jerked a large seax out of the guard's back, pushed him to the ground, and slit his throat.

"Gerwulf, you must run now," he whispered, quickly cutting my bonds. "There is little time."

I moved stiffly, rubbing my joints. Every part of my body throbbed as I tried to stand. He helped me stand and gave the guard's spear and his cloak.

"Brother, you risk too much," I said, covering myself.

"Not at all." He lowered his cowl. "God has finally talked to me, and this time he spoke with the voice of the old pagan gods. He told me what I had to do—whispered it right in here." He pointed to his ear and flashed me his madman's grin. "Now you must go. Escape this place. It is cursed by God and Wodan alike."

"What has happened?" I asked.

He paused and sat hard on the ground. "The King has turned the Saxons' surrender into a blood court. There is no justice here, only revenge," he said. "Not a single man out of more than four thousand was willing to betray Widukind, and the King cut off every one of their heads."

I grabbed his shoulders tightly and shook him. "What about the woman? Did you see the Saxon woman they captured?"

"Woman? No. There were no women, just peasant men and warriors."

"She is a warrior."

"Who is she? What is she to you—?" Pyttel stopped, searching my face for the answer he already knew.

I looked up. "She flies through the sky as the Raven."

"The Eater of Souls? The witch?"

"She is Vala, warrior, healer, and the Chooser of the Living and the Slain. She is the Walkyrie, and she chose life, for me and for the child she carries—our child."

He cackled. "And they call me mad! But they could not have captured her if she truly is a Walkyrie."

"I saw her, battered and bleeding like a mortal! They caught her with a noose and dragged her."

"Perhaps she came to you in a vision."

I put my hand on his shoulder. "I will not know until I find her."

He scratched his matted tonsure. "I heard that a few Saxons broke through the shield wall and fled into the forest, but—"

I smiled, cracking the crusts of dried blood and dirt on my cheeks. "Thank you, my friend. Thank you!" I embraced him tightly. "I will likely never see you again in this life or the next, but I will never forget you."

"I will sacrifice to Wodan for you, her, and your child."

I pulled away and did not look back as I ducked behind some hedges and skirted the field. I knew he was watching me fade into the night, babbling to both the Christian God and the pagan gods for my safety. Perhaps, they would fate us to meet again someday.

Torches and fires threw flickering light on massive piles of heads and beheaded bodies. They were heaped high across the King's field of bloody vengeance. They stood as morbid trophies for a tyrant, like the masses of wolf hides he had collected. Black ravens swarmed over the heads, plucking eyes from pallid gray faces with twisted mouths. I looked desperately from pile to pile of heads. I was too far away to see the faces clearly, and most were bloodied beyond recognition.

I would not find her there. There was only one place to search for her, to find the truth, to find myself.

The Raven's Stones.

If she was alive, she would be there—no other place for hope or no better place to die.

I followed the meandering Weser River through the flatlands and bogs. I ran through the night and into the next day. The ground dried as I entered the Teutoburg Forest, and I cut straight south. My body ached from the beating I had taken, but ground was soft under my feet, and the woodland air was fresh and crisp. It smelled of freedom.

So many things were clear to me now. I understood why I could not pray in gratitude and why God did not hear my prayers. I was not grateful for anything God had done. He did not come to hearten me when I had lain tied and bound, enduring the agony of wounds in the stone chamber. When I suffered the madness of captivity, He had not come to me to bestow strength and courage. He had watched me struggle to overcome by myself. He had abandoned me as He had when I suffered flogging and banishment as a child.

Vala had stayed with me, holding me, healing me, loving me. She had always been near.

The Raven who spoke to the wolf in me
The Walkyrie who challenged me
…and the woman who stole my heart
Vala

I watched the sky closely for any sign of the Raven, but saw none. Fatigue and hunger slowed me, but I did not stop to rest. By the next day, I was nearing the Raven's Stones. The Wulf-hednar might be there, expecting me, waiting in ambush. They might kill me or they might embrace me. Enchantments in the forest could entangle me in thorns or drown me in a quagmire, but none of these threats frightened me. Nothing terrified me more than the thought of losing her.

I reached the base of the stones, next to the pool where we had swum naked. It was deadly quiet. I strained my ears but did not hear the slightest breeze in the trees nor the sound of a mouse scampering through the grass. The place was deserted.

Weak and dizzy from pain, hunger, and thirst, I climbed the stairs carved into the rock. They wound around the giant stone a long way, more than the height of twenty men. I tried to run but stumbled several times. At the top, I found the plank set in place, crossing the gap to great pillar, the sacred Irminsul that held up the skies. With my last scrap of energy, I crossed it into the stone chamber.

It was empty except for the altar under the little round window. Every morning, Vala had watched the sun rise through the window, waiting for the day when I would be healed and could join the Wulfhednar.

Upon the altar lay a fur, a wolf fur. My wolf skin. She had left it for me.

I threw it on and pulled the wolf's head over my own. I smelled her scent buried deep within and inhaled it greedily. For a moment, I felt her warm touch caring for me, her strong arms fighting me, and her soft skin next to mine. The scent faded quickly, and I could not recapture it. I looked around frantically and paced across the stone floor—waiting. It seemed hours passed, but it might have been only moments.

She was not here. She was not coming.

I collapsed to my knees and cursed God. "I damn you with all the pain you have given me! Send me to Hell! It could be no worse than what you have done to me."

I dragged myself to the door, as I had done when I had been nearly dead, when trying to escape from her. I had not understood her and had thought her a witch.

I would have given my right arm to return to that day, but it was too late. There was no warrior to challenge me, no Walkyrie to carry my soul, no woman to love me.

I tore the plank bridge out of the threshold and threw it. It tumbled and splinted on the sheer rock below. I imagined my bones breaking on the stone in the same way. I did not fear it. There was no pain as great as the tearing of my soul and my shattered heart.

I wavered on the edge of the threshold, hoping to fall, waiting for some unseen hand to push me. The ground far below was a blur of grasses and brush. I choked on my tears in despair, unable to live but unable to die. Weeping erupted from within and echoed off the stone walls. It was answered by a cry from outside, distant and faint at first. The cry grew into a powerful shriek and was soon accompanied by a familiar flutter of wings and the scent for which I hungered, the scent that gave me life.

Sweet musk and hawthorn

She was there. She was with me.

The Raven flew into the little round window and perched there. I pulled away from the edge of the doorway and crossed the chamber. She hopped onto my arm, tilting her head as she gazed at me. I stroked her sleek feathers, and her eyes remained black as night.

She was the Raven, and I was the Wulfhedinn.

I raised my arm to release her, and she flew through the little round window, soaring into the sky.

Historical Note

Return of the Wulfhedinn and book one in the Wulfhedinn series, *Feast of the Raven*, are set against the historical backdrop of the Saxon Wars in eighth-century Northern Germany. The major events of the campaign were based on research, including the disastrous ambush of the Frankish troops by the rebel Saxons and Charlemagne's bloody revenge at Verden.

Many of the major characters are real people from history. They include King Karl, later known as Charlemagne, General Theoderic, Brother Pyttel, Horse Master Gallo, Chamberlain Adalgis, Count Worad, and Prince Pepin. The locations in the novel still exist today in Germany. They include the towns of Paderborn, Lippespringe, Eresburg, and Verden, as well as the Hohenstein Plateau.

The Wulfhedinn and the Walkyrie are based on Germanic pagan traditions and beliefs of the time. The Raven's Stones, better known as the Externsteine, still stand in the Teutoburg

Forest near the town of Horn-Bad Meinberg, Germany. They are as shrouded in mystery today as they were in Charlemagne's time. It was while visiting this magical place that my fictional characters, Gerwulf and Vala, came alive. They have been with me ever since.

You can learn more about the historical and mythological elements of the Wulfhedinn Series on my blog at https://catherinespader.com/.